W9-CIL-115

### *"I'm not trying to hurt you,"*

Travis said.

"You are, and you know you are," Abbey answered.

"*We've* hurt each other," he countered sharply. "We have always hurt each other. Why do we do it?"

She looked past him, out the door. "I don't know," she finally replied. "But maybe that old adage applies."

"Which one?"

Her gaze pierced him. "The one that says familiarity breeds contempt."

"Contempt?" he repeated. "Contempt on whose part?"

"Yours."

Her rapid breathing and the movement of her breasts under her silk blouse belied her outward calmness. His reaction was startling—his need for her grew into pure physical hunger.

"Never contempt," he said slowly.

Dear Reader,

Welcome to Silhouette Romance—experience the magic of the wonderful world where two people fall in love. Meet heroines who will make you cheer for their happiness, and heroes (be they the boy next door or a handsome, mysterious stranger) who will win your heart. Silhouette Romance reflects the magic of love—sweeping you away with books that will make you laugh and cry; heartwarming, poignant stories that will move you time and time again.

In the next few months, we're publishing romances by many of your all-time favorites such as Diana Palmer, Brittany Young, Annette Broadrick and many others. Your response to these authors and others in Silhouette Romance has served as a touchstone for us, and we're pleased to bring you more books with Silhouette's distinctive medley of charm, wit and—above all—*romance*.

During 1991, we have many special events planned. Don't miss our WRITTEN IN THE STARS series. Each month in 1991, we're proud to present you with a book that focuses on the hero—and his astrological sign.

I hope you'll enjoy this book and all of the stories to come. Come home to romance—Silhouette Romance—for always!

Sincerely,

Tara Gavin
Senior Editor

## BOOKS THAT WILL HELP YOU GET ON IN THE WORLD

*It's sometimes tough to be a person in today's world. There are all sorts of pressures from jobs, institutions and society that everyone must face. Books can help you deal with these problems. And Pocket Books has the very finest books on the subject—books written by experts for every reader.*

| | | |
|---|---|---|
| ____ | 41844 | ART OF SELFISHNESS David Seabury $2.50 |
| ____ | 83118 | EXPLORING THE CRACK IN THE COSMIC EGG Joseph Chilton Pearce $2.50 |
| ____ | 81423 | HOW TO CURE YOURSELF OF POSITIVE THINKING Donald G. Smith $1.50 |
| ____ | 81734 | HOW TO NEGOTIATE A RAISE John Tarrant $1.75 |
| ____ | 41596 | HOW TO DEVELOP SELF-CONFIDENCE Dale Carnegie $2.50 |
| ____ | 41299 | HOW TO WIN FRIENDS & INFLUENCE PEOPLE Dale Carnegie $2.50 |
| ____ | 41491 | STAND UP! SPEAK OUT! TALK BACK! The Key to Self-Assertive Therapy. Robert E. Alberti & Michael Emmons $2.50 |
| ____ | 41444 | SUCCESS THROUGH A POSITIVE MENTAL ATTITUDE Napoleon Hill & W. C. Stone $2.75 |
| ____ | 41371 | UP FROM DEPRESSION Leonard Cammer, M.D. 2.50 |
| ____ | 82861 | RELEASE FROM NERVOUS TENSION David Harold Fink, M.D. $2.25 |
| ____ | 82184 | MANAGERIAL WOMAN Margaret Hennig & Anne Jardim $2.50 |
| ____ | 41761 | HOW TO ENJOY YOUR LIFE AND YOUR JOB Dale Carnegie $2.50 |
| ____ | 81910 | SYSTEMANTICS, John Gall $1.95 |

**POCKET BOOKS**
Department PPA
1230 Avenue of the Americas
New York, N.Y. 10020

Please send me the books I have checked above. I am enclosing $_____ (please add 50¢ to cover postage and handling for each order, N.Y.S. and N.Y.C. residents please add appropriate sales tax). Send check or money order—no cash or C.O.D.s please. Allow up to six weeks for delivery.

NAME_____

ADDRESS_____

CITY_____STATE/ZIP_____

14

# YOUR BODY & YOU

Do you know how much your body reveals about your thoughts, anxieties, personality? How important are the body's actions to mental well-being?
Find out with these popular books on the subject

from

## POCKET BOOKS

| | | | |
|---|---|---|---|
| \_\_\_\_\_ | 42069 | EVERYTHING YOU ALWAYS WANTED TO KNOW ABOUT ENERGY BUT WERE TOO WEAK TO ASK Naura Hayden | $2.50 |
| \_\_\_\_\_ | 83487 | BODYBUILDING FOR EVERYONE  Lou Ravelle | $1.95 |
| \_\_\_\_\_ | 80779 | BIORHYTHM  Arbie Dale, Ph.D | $1.75 |
| \_\_\_\_\_ | 41645 | BODY LANGUAGE  Julius Fast | $2.50 |
| \_\_\_\_\_ | 41849 | LANGUAGE OF FEELINGS  David Viscott | $2.25 |
| \_\_\_\_\_ | 41721 | LUSCHER COLOR TEST  Ian Scott, ed. | $2.75 |

**POCKET BOOKS**
**Department YBY**
**1230 Avenue of the Americas**
**New York, N.Y. 10020**

Please send me the books I have checked above. I am enclosing $_____ (please add 50¢ to cover postage and handling for each order, N.Y.S. and N.Y.C. residents please add appropriate sales tax). Send check or money order—no cash or C.O.D.s please. Allow up to six weeks for delivery.

NAME_____

ADDRESS_____

CITY_____STATE/ZIP_____

38

# MARCINE SMITH

# The Two of Us

Published by Silhouette Books New York

America's Publisher of Contemporary Romance

For Daryl

**SILHOUETTE BOOKS**
300 E. 42nd St., New York, N.Y. 10017

THE TWO OF US

Copyright © 1990 by Marcine C. Smith

All rights reserved. Except for use in any review,
the reproduction or utilization of this work in
whole or in part in any form by any electronic,
mechanical or other means, now known or
hereafter invented, including xerography,
photocopying and recording, or in any information
storage or retrieval system, is forbidden without
the permission of Silhouette Books, 300 E. 42nd St.,
New York, N.Y. 10017

ISBN: 0-373-08767-5

First Silhouette Books printing January 1991

All the characters in this book are fictitious. Any
resemblance to actual persons, living or dead, is
purely coincidental.

®: Trademark used under license and
registered in the United States Patent and
Trademark Office and in other countries.

Printed in the U.S.A.

---

## MARCINE SMITH

taught high school until the birth of her youngest son, who has now graduated from high school. When she discovered she had neither the talent nor the inclination to be a full-time homemaker, she returned to college and took courses in anything that interested her, from clinical psychology to Egyptology. Now, Marcine and her husband have a farrowing-to-finishing operation in northwest Iowa that produces fifteen hundred hogs a year.

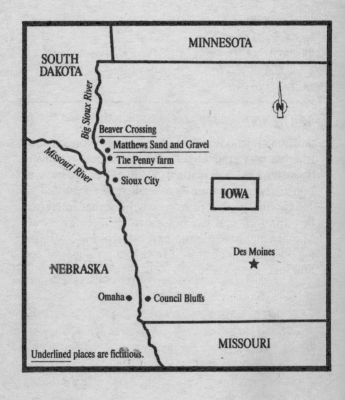

MINNESOTA

SOUTH DAKOTA

*Big Sioux River*

Beaver Crossing
● Matthews Sand and Gravel
● The Penny farm
● Sioux City

*Missouri River*

IOWA

Des Moines
★

NEBRASKA

Omaha ●  ● Council Bluffs

MISSOURI

Underlined places are fictitious.

# Prologue

Travis, his jeans rolled to his knees, stood calf-deep in Beaver Crossing Creek. He bent, picked up a pebble, straightened and looked to where Abbey sat on the bank putting on her sneakers.

She'd been wading and skipping pebbles with him until a few minutes ago, when she'd abruptly announced she had to get home to milk her cows, Daisy and Belinda, then fix supper for her father.

He waited until she finished tying her laces and glanced up before tossing the pebble sidearm. The pebble skipped over the surface twice, then sank, kicking up a puff of silt as it settled.

"Didn't go fifteen feet," he said, leaving the water to join her.

"It wasn't that bad," Abbey said.

Abbey had beaten him on every toss today, but Travis didn't mind as he would have a couple of years ago. He supposed it had to do with being almost thirteen and growing up.

He'd talked to Bobby Diller, the other boy in his and Abbey's class, about how Abbey seemed to be changing. Bobby had said he didn't see any changes in Abbey. Bobby thought all three girls in their class were stupid.

Abbey was mule-headed and weird. His cousin, Jill Fulbright, was stupid, even if she was smart. And Cassie Manning was the weirdest and stupidest of all, with a shape like a dipstick, to boot. Cassie was sweet on Bob, but Bob wasn't having anything to do with her. Not *that* way.

Travis wiped his hands on his jeans, then rolled the pant legs down. "You ever wanted to kiss a boy?" he asked, trying to act as though he wasn't really interested in her answer.

Abbey made a sour face. "The idea makes me gag."

Travis nodded as if he agreed the idea was repugnant, but lately he'd done a lot of thinking about kissing Abbey. He was pretty sure he'd like to try it. The problem was, he wasn't sure how to go about it. In the movies when a guy wanted to kiss a girl, he just grabbed her and kissed her. But he figured if he grabbed Abbey, she'd think he was practicing a new wrestling hold, and he figured his chances of her pinning him were better than his chances of kissing her.

"You ever wanted to kiss a girl?" Abbey asked.

"No," Travis said, sounding cross. "Why'd you ask me?"

"Well! Why'd you ask me?"

Abbey's voice had taken on a brittle crackle. Travis knew it wouldn't take much and she'd want to fight.

Impulsively he decided to test the water. "Guess if I had to kiss anyone it would be you."

"Yeah," she said. "Same with me. I guess if I had to kiss anyone it would be you."

Travis ran his feet sideways through the brome-grass to dry them. "I wish you didn't have to move into town," he said.

Abbey sighed. "Dad says he has to sell the farm because he doesn't have insurance. And the bills from Mother's operations were tremendous."

The farm in question was one Jen Baird inherited from her parents, the Pennys. Mr. Penny had inher-ited it from his parents. Jen's last operation had taken place a couple of months ago, but she wasn't better—she was worse. She didn't even do her seamstress work anymore.

Travis turned to face Abbey, pulling his legs up and wrapping his arms around them. Abbey mimicked his movement, so they sat kneecap to kneecap and eye to eye.

His folks had bought the farm next to the Penny place before he was born. He and Abbey had grown up together. "I'm going to miss you when you move into town," he said.

"I'm going to miss you, too," Abbey said. "But like Mother says, town's only a mile away, so I can visit the farm whenever I want, and once school starts we'll see each other every day at school."

"Sure," Travis said. "We'll see each other, but it won't be the same."

"Why would you say that?"

Why had he said it? Maybe because he'd remem-bered what his mother had said about Abbey's growing up to be a beauty and drawing boys to her like bees were drawn to honey.

"I don't know, Abbey. Maybe I said it wouldn't be the same because we'll be in high school," Travis said. "You'll get new friends. I'll get new friends. Like that."

"You'll always be my very best friend," Abbey said staunchly. "Even after I leave Beaver Crossing to go to college."

Travis pivoted away and grabbed a sneaker. "You still planning on being a fashion designer and living in New York or Paris?" he asked.

"Mother says I've got to go to college, make something of myself," Abbey said. "And I guess she's right. I can't do that if I stay in Beaver Crossing."

"Yeah," Travis said. "I've heard her tell you that."

"What are you going to do after we graduate from high school?" Abbey asked. "Go to college or stay here and help your dad run the sand and gravel business?"

Travis hadn't given much thought to what he was going to do after high school, and the way Abbey had asked made him feel that if he didn't say he was going to college, he was admitting he was planning on never amounting to anything.

"Dad says he wants to see our whole farm be like one big lake. And if the sand and gravel business gets that big, he'll need me to help him run it," Travis said. To cover all the bases, he added, "But maybe I'll go to college first."

"I don't feel quite so bad, knowing your dad bought our farm," Abbey said. She paused, her lips seeming to tremble. For a second Travis thought she was going to cry. "Because he promised Mother that when she gets to feeling better he'll sell the buildings back to us."

Suddenly Travis was angry. He didn't know why and whom he was angry with. Maybe it was with Abbey for growing up faster than he was. Maybe it was because she'd already made up her mind to leave Beaver Crossing and he hated the idea, and she didn't seem to hate it at all. Maybe it was because she acted as if she didn't know she had to move because of her old man.

"My dad bought the farm because he thinks there's gravel on it," he retorted heatedly. "And he's giving your dad a job at the pit because he feels sorry for you and your mother."

"That isn't true!"

"The hell it ain't true," Travis growled. "Everyone feels sorry for you and your mom, because everyone knows Lemont isn't selling the Penny place because Jen's sick and he had bills to pay. He's selling it because Jen's too sick to keep things going."

Abbey gnawed her lip. "He'll pay the bills. He promised Mother."

Travis slipped on the second sneaker, made furious motions in tying it and cursed when it knotted. "Your dad's a drunk, Abbey," he snapped. "He'll drink up whatever he lays his hands on."

Abbey's gaze was on him like the teeth of an angry dog. She shoved herself to standing, hovered over him. "I ought to pound in your face!"

Travis reluctantly rose to confront her. She was four inches taller than he and he had to look up to meet her gaze and try to look mean at the same time. It wasn't easy, not because she towered over him, but because in his heart he knew he shouldn't be mean to her. She couldn't help it if Lemont was a drunk.

But he wasn't backing down. "Go ahead. Take your best shot," he said.

Abbey, lips trembling, jerked her T-shirt down over her hips, tightening the thin white material over her chest. Travis gulped. Her breasts stood out like small balloons.

"You're a stinker, Travis Mathews," she said. "You think you're so high and mighty. I can hardly wait to leave Beaver Crossing, just to get away from you!"

With all the dignity she could muster, Abbey turned her back on the only real friend she'd ever had. Every word Travis had said was true, but he had no right to say them.

She crawled through the barbed wire into the pasture to take the shortcut home. Huge sobs tore through her body. Her mother was dying. She'd wanted to tell Travis, but she was glad she hadn't. She hated him. She should have punched him out.

"Abbey! Run!"

Abbey turned at Travis's screams. Her dad's Holstein bull had stopped grazing. He was sniffing the air and pawing the ground, kicking up a dirt mist. Abbey's mind told her to run, but her legs wouldn't go.

The bull charged. Travis, waving a dead tree branch, raced to intervene. It happened so fast. Travis swung, caught the bull behind his foreleg. The bull stumbled. Travis dropped the branch, grabbed her hand, wheeled her around and dragged her with him.

They sprinted to the nearest tree. Travis shoved Abbey, so she could shimmy up the tree to grab the first thick limb. Then she helped him up. By the time they were squared away, legs dangling, the bull stood beneath the tree, looking up, snorting.

"Wonder how long he'll stand there?" Abbey asked breathlessly.

"Until he gets tired," Travis said.

Their laughter pealed across the pasture, then faded to snickering. "You know what, Travis?" Abbey asked. "You really and truly are my very best friend."

"You're mine, too," Travis said. "Want to make a promise that no matter what, we'll be best friends forever?"

"Promise," Abbey said.

# Chapter One

Abbey switched the handset from one ear to the other. "Maxine. This is Abigail Baird. How are you?"

"Fine," the woman said. "It's freezing in New York. How's the weather in Minneapolis?"

"Warm for this early in April." They visited briefly, then Abbey said, "Reports from our store manager say the spring-summer line of Bella Sports is outselling expectations."

"That's encouraging news," Maxine said.

Abbey came straight to the point. "At this late date is there a chance of boosting my order on the fall inventory?"

Abbey was confident Maxine would do what she could to supply what was needed for the Hesston chain. Bella Sports was a new fashion house. Until Abbey, head buyer for the Hesston stores, had placed

Bella Sports in their stores, the main outlet for the small company had been specialty shops.

Maxine asked for specifics. Abbey read from the list she'd compiled, pausing after each item to allow Maxine to make notes. Maxine said she'd check with production and sales and get back pronto.

As Abbey returned the handset to the receiver, her secretary of three months breezed into the office, carrying a stack of mail.

"Don't tell me all that mail needs my personal attention," Abbey said.

Nicole grinned. "Sorry to say, but yes. Any luck with Maxine?"

"She's going to get back," Abbey said.

"You should have gone with your intuition and beefed up the inventory when you ordered the fall line," Nicole observed.

Abbey had started working for Daniel Hesston during the summer of her sophomore year at college. She'd returned each summer, gaining experience at different levels of management. After graduation, he'd offered her a position as assistant manager at one of the smaller stores. Six years later, she'd moved up the ladder to head buyer for the ten-store chain.

"Daniel didn't build his business by making intuitive decisions and impulsive purchases," Abbey said. "And all I had when I ordered the fall inventory was the gut feeling the Bella Sports line was going to be well received by our customers."

"I know," Nicole agreed easily. "I also knew when you said you had a hunch Bella Sports was going to be hot that you wouldn't go with your intuition."

"You did?" Abbey bantered.

"I did." Nicole piled the mail in a neat stack on the desk. When she straightened and looked at Abbey again, her expression was thoughtful. "I haven't known you long, but I've observed the way you work and I'm beginning to wonder whether you've ever done anything impulsive."

Ten years ago, Abbey reflected. Making love with Travis hadn't been thought out.

She shifted on the chair, brightened her expression. "As a matter of fact, I have done something impulsive," she said. "I fished you from the secretarial pool, didn't I?"

Nicole laughed. "Sure you did. After you spent two weeks thinking about it. By the way, while you were on the line with Maxine, a Cassandra Diller called and—"

"Cassie? Did she leave a message?"

Nicole frowned slightly. "I was coming to that."

"So sorry about the interruption."

"You're forgiven. Cassandra said she'll call back. And Evan Terrill called. He said he'll pick you up for dinner at eight."

"I'll have to cancel Evan," Abbey said. "Daniel hired a manager for the south side Hesston store. He's arranged a dinner tonight, so the rest of the managers and department heads can meet him."

"This is the third time this month that you've broken a date with Evan because Mr. Hesston threw some last-minute business meeting at you," Nicole observed.

Abbey had been dating Evan six months. She liked him immensely. Lately he'd begun making it clear that he would like to have their relationship more clearly defined.

"Evan will understand," she said.

"If Evan is *that* understanding, is there any possibility you're going to marry him?"

Abbey wanted marriage, but not yet. She hadn't achieved the career goals she'd set for herself. She thought a vice presidency position with Hesston was in the future. Maybe in the not too distant future.

"You constantly amaze me," Abbey needled.

Nicole nibbled her lip. "Okay. I'll bite. What about me constantly amazes you?"

"How reluctant you are to poke your nose into my personal life." Abbey smiled. "You ought to try to be less hesitant."

"I know one thing, Mr Hesston could never, under any circumstances, get me to pass up dinner with Evan for a business engagement," Nicole said. "That is, unless you're stalling Evan for some reason."

Smiling, Nicole swept from the office, closing the door behind her. Stalling Evan? Abbey wondered. No, she didn't think she was stalling. It was simply that at this point in her life, her career was top priority; when she did marry, marriage and family would come first.

But to be perfectly honest with herself, she was wary of personal commitment. If Travis had taught her one thing, it was not to place blind faith in anyone.

She drew the mail toward her. She'd read one letter, a second and a third when she began wondering why Cassie had called her at the office. It had to be something important, she decided.

She leaned forward and reached for the telephone. A moment later, a bubbling voice sang, "Diller resi-

dence. Cassie speaking. How have you been, Abbey?"

"What if it hadn't been me, but the president, calling to congratulate you on your contribution to the
betterment of womankind?" Abbey asked.

"Did the news that I married Bob reach the White
House so soon? It's only been four years."

"For two people who *loathed* each other right up to
your elopement, you've survived admirably," Abbey
said.

"Well," Cassie retorted, "you know how it is.
Bob's like a nasty-tempered pup, but so darn loveable
I feel obligated to care for him."

Abbey smiled. Cassie was a lab technician at a Sioux
City hospital. Bob, the youngest of the Diller family,
had taken over his parents' grocery store. He and
Cassie had spent a year remodeling an older house on
the north side of town and had recently moved into it.

In many ways, Abbey felt she'd outgrown Beaver
Crossing, but she'd never outgrown her friends. Cassie, Bob and Jill were a steady current in her life, well
loved and always there.

She would never deny her roots were in Beaver
Crossing, either, driven deep at the Penny place. She'd
never given up her dream of reclaiming the buildings.
A year might go by, two, then letters, telephone calls
and the visits of her friends to Minneapolis wouldn't
be enough. She would be drawn back to Beaver
Crossing, back to the farm.

Abbey asked about Cassie's parents. Bob's. Jill's.
Cassie said everyone was fine. She went on to say she'd
taken a week's vacation to settle the house and was

also attending auction sales, in hopes of picking up some older furniture she and Bob could refinish.

"Mother stored some good pieces in the shed at the farm," Abbey said. "I couldn't sell any of it, but there might be something you and Bob can use. Why don't you go out and take a look? If you see something you want, take it."

"I'd rather you were along," Cassie said.

"I've been thinking about using some of the furniture myself in the new apartment. We'll check the shed out the next time I'm back," Abbey said.

"I thought you weren't moving until next month."

"The painters finished early," Abbey said. "I was eager to get out of my cramped studio. Now I'm knocking around five rooms with barren spots and bare walls. I need a living-room set. A dining-room set." She sighed. "The works."

Cassie chuckled. "You sound so domestic."

Abbey laughed. "I wouldn't go that far," she said, "but there are a few things I'd like to have, now that I've the room for them. Like Mother's china, which is also stored in the shed."

"We'll definitely put a visit to the shed on our agenda," Cassie said. "And...ah...maybe you'd better plan to make it soon. Something has come up."

Cassie's serious tone frightened Abbey. "What's happened?" she asked.

"I hesitated to call," Cassie said. "This is...well, it's about Travis."

A shock wave washed through Abbey, then reverberated in a series of chilling surges. No matter what he'd done to her, she didn't want to think he could be ill or could have had an accident. And she knew Travis flew his own plane.

"He had an accident with the plane," she murmured.

"No. Nothing like that," Cassie said. "He was here last night and while we were visiting, he mentioned that he was going to raze the buildings on the Penny place."

Abbey's stomach cramped. "Raze the buildings! When?"

"In two weeks a crew is going to start the salvage. When they're done, the bulldozers will level what's left," Cassie said. "I thought you might want to take one last look at the place."

Abbey's mind was working furiously. She had talked to Roy Matthews last fall. He knew she still wanted the building site.

"I need to talk to Roy," she said. "I'll call him right—"

"Roy and Christina left this week on a cruise. I understand they'll be gone for a month."

"Then I'll have to deal with Travis."

"Deal with him?" Cassie asked. "What are you talking about?"

"You know Roy promised my mother she could buy the buildings back. The only reason I haven't made an offer on the place was because I didn't have the ready money. I still don't, but I'll come up with it somehow."

"That was a long time ago, Abbey," Cassie murmured. "And what would you do with a bunch of old buildings, anyway?"

"What I do with them isn't important," Abbey said. "Saving them is. Roy hasn't forgotten. Travis can't—" she was saying, when a flashing light indicated an incoming call. Likely to be Maxine. "I've got an incoming call. I'll see you sometime tomorrow."

"Tomorrow?"

"I'll leave Minneapolis by five in the morning. I should be in Beaver Crossing by ten."

They said goodbye quickly. Abbey, scowling from the unsettling nature of Cassie's call, switched to the waiting call. It was from Maxine. The woman informed Abbey that she would be getting most of the inventory she'd requested.

The moment the call ended and Abbey's mind was free of business, a feeling of haplessness came over her. Travis might have forgotten a lot of things about her, but he couldn't have forgotten how she felt about the Penny place.

So why was he doing this?

She'd gathered from her friends that Travis had become aggressive in expanding the business; that it had been he, not Roy, who'd turned the small sand and gravel operation into a multimillion-dollar empire by buying every farm in the valley that had sand and gravel on it. The Matthews owned over a thousand acres of Big Sioux bottom land.

So why did he have to mess with the few acres the Penny buildings occupied?

Why? The answer was simple. Because he *was* Travis, accustomed to having things *his* own way.

Travis had been her best friend, the only one she'd trusted with her most intimate thoughts. He'd been the one who'd stood by her when her mother died, and her tears had sprung from a well of grief so deep that she'd believed she would never stop crying. She'd told Travis how alone she felt. Travis had told her that he was there. She wasn't alone. And he'd made her feel she wasn't.

He'd been the one who'd listened when she lamented how she detested the whispers labeling her father the town drunk and herself "poor Abbey." He'd told her not to listen, that the opinions of other people didn't matter.

He'd held her when her father died. She'd cried again. Only the tears were tears of guilt. She hadn't loved her father, hadn't respected him. Travis had assured her that she wasn't heartless for not loving her father. He'd assured her that she was warm and loving. He needed her, he'd said. Marry me, he'd said.

But she'd had obligations, debts. Travis had been right. Her father had never paid the medical expenses incurred during her mother's illness. When her father had developed cirrhosis of the liver, the insurance Roy had carried on him had covered most of the medical expenses, but she'd been left with the burial costs. And she'd had to plan for college.

She'd told him the timing wasn't right.

A scant three months later he wasn't asking her to marry him. He was asking whether or not she was pregnant, and when she said no, he'd said, "Then I guess I'm not obligated to you, am I?"

Abbey pushed herself from reverie.

For ten years she and Travis had purposefully avoided each other. At first the avoidance, at least on her part, had been because she'd known it would hurt too much to see him. Even thinking about him had caused anguish.

Now she didn't feel anything. She didn't care what he did with his personal life. She didn't even care whether he dug the pit to the back porch of the house. But he wasn't going one damned foot farther.

## Chapter Two

The compelling idea that she had nothing to lose and everything to gain by confronting her old nemesis lost its appeal during the drive to Beaver Crossing. By the time Abbey turned off the highway and headed toward the pit, all the festering aches and anxieties she thought she'd put to rest had flared.

She reminded herself that she was not the same person who'd been desperately in love with Travis and desperately in need of his love. She didn't need his approval anymore. Or his respect. So he couldn't hurt her.

The office parking lot was crowded. Employees, she surmised. She located the designated visitors' spaces in front of the building and parked.

No expense had been spared in either the new, low cedar-shingled brick building or the landscaping around it. The Matthewses had achieved a pleasing look in harmony with the countryside.

She realized she was procrastinating! How pleasing the building was or wasn't was irrelevant. Either Travis was inside or he wasn't. That was what was relevant.

A smiling young woman looked up as Abbey stepped into the reception area. "Abbey! What a surprise!"

It took Abbey a moment to recognize the dark-haired young lady as Clara Green's great niece. Abbey's parents had rented Clara Green's bungalow when they moved into town.

Abbey extended her hand. "Meg Parker! The last time I saw you, you were in grade school, weren't you?"

Meg smiled, offered her hand. "I graduated from high school last year," she said cheerfully. "I attend the University of South Dakota and work here every Saturday."

There couldn't be more than nine years' difference in their ages, Abbey reflected. But she wondered if she'd ever been that young.

"I remember when I saw you last," Abbey said. "Clara had broken her hip and you and your mother came to visit her."

When Abbey's father died, Clara had insisted that Abbey move in with her, sleeping in what was called the cherry bedroom. She'd been living with Clara when the old lady fell from a ladder, while trying to dust the dining-room chandelier.

Clara had been married once. Rumor had it that Tom Green had deserted Clara shortly after their marriage because of Clara's "nasty" temper, and had died without ever returning to Beaver Crossing.

"Have you seen Aunt Clara?" Meg asked.

"I talked with her on the phone a couple of weeks ago," Abbey said.

"You always stop to visit her when you're in town, don't you?"

"I always do. I'll go there later today," Abbey said. "She's all right, isn't she?"

"She's fine," Meg said. "She says she feels more chipper at eighty-five than she did at seventy…but I thought you might like to know that her husband is back."

"Her husband? I thought he'd died years ago."

"So did I. So did my folks. So did everyone, I guess. Naturally when Aunt Clara called and said, 'Tommy's come home,' Mother rushed right over, thinking Aunt Clara'd fallen and hit her head on the bathtub or something. You know. Hallucinating."

Abbey was too amazed to do more than make noises in place of comment. The man had to have been gone sixty years.

"But there he was, just like Aunt Clara said, sitting with her on the davenport," Meg said. "Mother said they were holding hands and kissing each other. Both showing signs of senility in Mother's opinion."

Abbey found her voice. "It must have been a shock to Clara," she said. "Thinking all those years that her husband was dead."

"That's another thing," Meg said. "It turns out that Aunt Clara didn't know whether he'd died or not. She says that after Tommy left, she got tired of people asking whether she'd heard from him, so she started telling them that as far as she knew, he'd died. He went to Canada. That's where he's been living."

"For heaven's sake," Abbey murmured.

"My folks think it's weird," Meg said pensively. "Him showing up, moving right in. They think he's after her money or something. But I think it's beautiful. Don't you?"

"I think that if Clara and Tom are happy, then it's nobody's business," she said.

"Right," Meg agreed emphatically. "And now, what can I do for you?"

Maybe it was the quick switch Meg made in the conversation, but once she'd asked what Abbey wanted, Abbey had to fight the inclination to turn tail and run. She took herself firmly in hand. "I'd like to speak to Travis," she said, "if he's available."

"Down the hall, past the office where the girls are working, second door on your right," Meg said, gesturing in that direction. "He's alone. Just walk in."

"Thank you," Abbey said.

She managed a deliberate stride down the hall, but was almost intimidated by her surroundings, the plush, green carpet, the barn-wood paneling on the walls. The impressive prints, she knew, had cost a bundle.

She passed one closed door. Second on the right. No need to get tense, she told herself. Enough time had passed, so that it would be like meeting a stranger. She'd be able to deal with Travis objectively, dispassionately.

Travis didn't look up from his work when the rap sounded on the door. An hour ago he'd called down to the scale house to tell the pit supervisor to send Neal

Noteboom to the office. Noteboom had taken his sweet time arriving. Understandable. The man had to know he was going to be fired.

"Come in," Travis said. When the door opened but didn't close, he glanced up, then felt as if a blow had been delivered to his stomach, forcing the air from his lungs. His heart stopped beating. When it started again, the beat was erratic.

She was as beautiful as he'd remembered, but like the image on a photo, time had blurred the sharpness of the details in his memory. He hadn't remembered that her cheekbones were quite so wide, her jawline so delicate or her brown eyes so deep-set.

She'd reached five foot eight by the end of their freshman year. About the time he'd given up hope of catching her, he'd had a spurt in growth. By the end of their sophomore year he'd caught Abbey, passed her. Then her body had fitted intimately to his six-foot frame.

Her figure had matured. She was full-breasted, lean-ribbed, small-waisted, and looked every inch the executive she was, wearing a dark blue suit and light blue blouse. No frills, just elegance. But cold.

Or was the coldness in her demeanor? She was regarding him in a circumspect manner. Why not? He'd told her nothing would make him happier than never seeing her again. And at the time he'd damn well meant it.

"Hello, Travis," she said.

It was hard for him to get around the soothing alto of her voice to see the wariness and distrust in her eyes. But she didn't have the corner on those emotions.

Belatedly he wondered what she wanted. Abbey wouldn't be here unless she wanted something.

"What brings you?" he asked.

She glanced at a chair. "Mind if I sit?"

"Sure." Her eyes snapped at him. He half chuckled. "I meant what the heck, have a chair. Not that I minded whether or not you made yourself comfortable."

Abbey closed the door, walked to the straight-backed chair closest to her—farthest from him—and settled on the leather seat. His blue-eyed gaze had lost none of its mesmerizing quality. But the rest of him, the range, the bulk and breadth of him beneath a crewneck, gray jersey and denims had matured. Nicely, she grudgingly admitted.

The stern set of his jaw and the premature touch of gray at his temples were startling. She hadn't envisioned Travis graying at twenty-eight. Of course, she hadn't envisioned him as an honest-to-God millionaire, either. Of the two of them, she'd been the one with drive.

Overall, her first reaction was one of relief. Ten years had changed him. This was not the young man she'd loved. This man really was a stranger.

Still, she couldn't talk to him as she would have to a stranger, and she wondered what she *could* say to him. It was irrational to think they could engage in chitchat, or talk about themselves as they'd been. Equally bizarre to pretend they'd *never* been.

She'd already bungled by not telling him what she wanted when he'd asked, but at that point all she'd had in mind was sitting, before he became aware that she was shaking. She'd come directly to the point when he gave her a second opportunity, she decided.

Which it appeared he was in no hurry to do. He'd settled back in his chair and was regarding her candidly. If he was searching for some flaw to single out, he wouldn't find it. She'd stopped at Jake's gas station and used the rest-room mirror to freshen her makeup and brush through her hair.

Stare to your heart's content, she thought. This isn't like old times. You can't make me squirm.

As if he'd read the message in the eye game she was playing, he smiled. Abbey's heart lurched, then raced, before she reminded herself that he'd always used his smile like a lure, taking her in before lowering the boom.

"How have you been?" he asked, then smiled again.

"Fine," she said. Her voice had sounded forced, dry. In spite of herself she was tense. Understandable. Her world had once orbited around him. She cleared her throat. "Wonderful. And you?"

"Fine. Wonderful," he said. "And from time to time I've thought about you."

"I won't ask if they were pleasant thoughts," she said.

"Some were undeniably pleasant," he stated softly.

A feeling of tenderness came over Abbey, as a few, undeniably pleasant memories of her own swirled in her mind. But she wasn't here to remember sweet thoughts.

"I'd be lying if I said I've never thought about you. Naturally, something happens on occasion that triggers a memory," she said. "Most recently yesterday, when Cassie called to tell me you were planning to raze my place."

"The Penny place isn't your place," Travis said.

In response to the dangerously weighted tone of his voice, Abbey was immediately vigilant. "You have a point," she said, forcing herself to convey confidence. "I should have said that I want the buildings and I'm prepared to buy them from you."

Anger ripped through Travis. He'd known she wouldn't have come to him if she hadn't wanted something. She'd never *needed* him unless she wanted something.

When he'd asked Abbey to marry him, she'd wanted to "get on with her life." Later, when she feared pregnancy, she'd wanted to marry him. When she discovered she wasn't carrying his child, she'd called it "lucky," because she wanted to get on with her life.

Now she was back, still saying, "I want" and expecting acquiescence from him. But she wasn't getting it. He should have cleared the land of the buildings a long time ago. He didn't know why he hadn't.

"I have plans for the place. Do you?" he asked.

"Of course," Abbey said. "I've decided—"

"You've decided to come back to Beaver Crossing?" he interrupted rudely, knowing she would never come back. Not when she'd been so driven to escape it. Escape him.

"I thought I'd restore the buildings and—"

"You want to use the place as a vacation retreat," he stated sarcastically. "Not a bad idea. A small, freshwater lake within walking distance. And I suppose you'd like to buy a few acres of pasture so you could keep a few horses."

He knew he was being mean, but he couldn't help himself. When she failed to answer, he sharpened his attack. "Or do you want the Penny place to show people Abigail Penny-Baird has made something of herself? That she's someone to be respected?"

For a long moment they dropped the pretense of civility and openly warred with their eyes, filled with grievances and gibes.

"Well, Abbey," he said, "no answer?"

Her expression changed again. Pain exploded in her brown eyes, reached across the room and slammed him in the chest. Her lips trembled. He'd gone too far.

"I have never thought of Beaver Crossing or the people with contempt. And no matter how contemptuously you treat me," she said, her voice breaking, "I'm not going to get into an exchange of accusations with you. You know I love the Penny place. And you know that's the reason I want it."

Travis sighed. He'd wanted to knife through her armor of poise, to hurt her—and he had. But there was no satisfaction in discovering she was vulnerable. Only remorse and a lesson relearned: when Abbey hurt, he hurt worse.

"I'm sorry, Abbey. That was a cheap shot. I know you love the place."

Abbey believed that at the moment he was sorry, but she couldn't trust him. "I want to restore the buildings and rent them out," she said.

"Have you seen the place recently?" he asked.

Abbey knew the point Travis was trying to make. "I visit the farm every time I'm in Beaver Crossing. I know the buildings are in need of repair, but I'm willing to spend whatever it takes to restore them."

"Restoration of the buildings would be a waste of money," he said.

"Is that it?" Abbey asked. "You're refusing my offer because you think it would be a waste of money?"

Travis leaned forward, intent. "I'm telling you that before I built my house, I considered restoration of the buildings on the Penny place, because living there would have put me closer to work. But the buildings are structurally unsound."

"The buildings don't look unsound to me," Abbey stated flatly.

"You aren't an architect."

"You are?" Abbey snapped.

"I've had an architect look at them. Have you?"

Trying to reason with Travis when he was in one of his I-know-all-the-answers moods was pointless, Abbey reflected. She'd have to talk to Roy.

"Could I ask a favor?"

"For old times' sake?" He grinned.

She ignored his attempt to render her thoughtless with that smile. She wasn't going to be outmaneuvered.

"I understand Roy and Christina are on a cruise. Will you hold off your plans until I've contacted Roy?"

"Be warned, Abbey," he said. "It won't do you any good to talk to Dad. He won't go against my decision. Everything else aside, the buildings are a hazard. They have to go."

"The shed, too?" Abbey asked through tight lips.

"The shed your mother used for storage?" he asked.

Abbey nodded, too angry with him to trust herself to speak. Didn't he remember anything? He'd helped her carry the smaller pieces of furniture and boxes from the house to the shed.

"Eventually, yes," he said. "Everything will go. I'm sorry, Abbey. I really am."

Blinded by fury, Abbey rose and walked to the door. Bitter words of recrimination battled her pressed lips to be spoken. But that wasn't the way. She needed a few hours to think. She forced a smile, turned back.

"It's been—"

"Nice to see me?" he asked.

"No," Abbey said.

"Interesting?"

"That pretty much describes it," Abbey agreed. "I haven't given up, Travis. I don't want to leave you with the impression that I have."

"I didn't think you had," Travis said. "You never gave up when it was something you wanted."

"As I recall, you didn't, either."

"I never gave up easily," he responded pointedly. "But when the odds were stacked against me, I had sense enough to accept it."

Damn him, Abbey thought viciously. The odds were not stacked against her. Not yet! She jerked open the door, nearly running into a young man in her rush to leave.

"Excuse me," she said. She brushed past him into the hall.

Travis noted the hungry look on Noteboom's face as his gaze followed Abbey. He didn't like it. But then, he didn't much like Noteboom.

"Step in and close the door," he said.

The young man allowed his gaze to linger on Abbey, then slowly responded to the order. Travis didn't offer Noteboom a chair. Their discussion was going to be short. He didn't have the patience his father had for men who weren't responsible, men like Lemont Baird.

Lemont couldn't be trusted to drive one of the trucks, so Roy had had him work as a handyman, doing odd jobs. Countless times, Roy had found Lemont drinking on the job. He'd threaten to fire him, but never had, because of Abbey.

"How long have you been with Matthews Sand and Gravel, Noteboom?" Travis asked. "Two months?"

"About that."

"And in that time you've collected how many speeding tickets?"

"Two."

"And what did I tell you after the last one?"

"That if I got another one, I was done driving for you," Noteboom said defiantly.

"And yesterday you were clocked at seventy-five with a loaded tandem—"

"It wasn't my fault," Noteboom interjected. "The speedometer on that truck I was driving was broke." Surly-faced, he slipped his hands into his jeans pockets.

"If you knew the speedometer wasn't working, it was your responsibility to report it to one of the mechanics," Travis stated. "You'll get two weeks' severance. Pick it up and whatever else I owe you on your way out. Make it fast enough so the door doesn't catch you on the backside when you close it."

When Noteboom left, Travis swore beneath his breath. He wouldn't tolerate his drivers risking lives, but he didn't enjoy firing anyone.

Normally he would have used more tact, but the encounter with Abbey had left him emotionally wiped out. Even when he'd been dealing with Noteboom, his mind had been on her, on how he'd grieved when she'd left him to "make something out of herself."

He'd been a long time burying the past, but he'd finally reached the point where he didn't cringe, yearn and ache every time someone mentioned her name.

Then he'd begun the search to replace her. He hadn't had much success and he'd wondered why. As Abbey stood framed in the doorway before entering the office, he'd known instantaneously what had been lacking in his relationships with other women. It was the connectedness he'd felt with Abbey....

But he still didn't understand why the sight of her caused the cords of his heart to strum wildly. Why, when she'd hurt him and his gaze settled on her trembling lips, the flood of memories washed over him.

Memories? He had a million of them. But in the end the memories were more bitter than sweet, more hostile than warm. And what stuck in his mind was how—when all he'd ever wanted to do was protect her—she'd hurt him.

The telephone rang. At first Travis stared at it as if he begrudged the interruption of his musing. But he didn't resent the distraction, he welcomed it.

He picked up the handset. "Travis speaking."

"Travis. This is Cassie. Is Abbey—?"

"I'll save you the trouble of warning me that Abbey is in town," Travis said. "She's been here and gone."

"I wasn't calling to warn you," Cassie said. "I was trying to locate her, to tell her to be sure to come here for lunch. Was she headed into town?"

"She didn't say," Travis said.

"Darn," Cassie murmured. "Jill flew home to spend the weekend with her folks. She'll be here for lunch. And Bob, of course." She hesitated. "Interested in coming?"

"I'd love to cross words with our favorite know-it-all," he said, "but no."

"Do you realize how difficult you and Abbey have made it for the rest of us over the years?" Cassie asked. "It's like a divorce, where the parties have decided to show everyone how civil they can be and no one believes it one little bit."

"Under the circumstances, civility sounds better to me than fighting," Travis said.

"Oh, sure," Cassie said bitingly. "It's loads of fun. When we're with you, we have to remember to watch what we say about Abbey. When we're with Abbey we're tripping over our tongues, watching what we say about you."

"I sympathize, but the situation is unavoidable."

"Nuts," Cassie said tersely. "The two of you act as if you're the only two people in the world who have ever had trouble."

"Get off the soapbox," Travis warned.

"I'm off it," Cassie snapped. "If Abbey happens to show up again, tell her about lunch."

The phone clicked in his ear.

Easygoing Cassie mad? Travis wondered as he returned the handset to the cradle. He thought for a minute about calling her back and apologizing. But apologize for what? He hadn't asked for advice. He didn't need advice.

The only way to live with Abbey was to live without her.

## Chapter Three

Although Abbey intended to go to the farm, she planned to do it after lunch. But she found it impossible to drive past the lane twice. While she was there, she'd take a quick inventory of the furniture stored in the shed, she decided. That way she could tell Cassie what was there.

She parked in front of the house and stepped from the car. The house was a bit of England sitting in northwest Iowa. Her great-great-grandparents had built it from plans they'd brought with them when they emigrated from England. How could Travis even consider getting rid of it?

As she walked across the lawn, the heels of her pumps sank through the bluegrass into the soft sod, making walking difficult. She stopped, propped her hand on her hip and studied the house.

Several rotted porch pillars that her father had never gotten around to replacing had finally given way. The porch roof sagged, shingles had slipped or been blown out of place. More shingles had risen on the main roof. She didn't need an expert to tell her that the rafters had pulled from the ridge beams.

The house had two main chimney stacks. Both had lost bricks, which were now strewn across the roof. Every window had panes missing.

It was in miserable shape. But it was still *home*.

Just as it had been when her mother was alive. No matter how short the money, her mother had always managed to buy sale material. She'd sew bright curtains, whip up sofa covers and braid rugs from scraps left over from her numerous dressmaking jobs. With those colorful rugs scattered around the house, it hadn't mattered that the linoleum was worn and cracked.

The bungalow in town had never been home to Abbey. Her mother had been too sick to do more than supervise as Abbey had sewn curtains, hung them and arranged the furniture.

After her mother died, Abbey had cooked, cleaned house, done the laundry and waited for her father to appreciate her efforts. He never had. The bungalow, with the potential to be a home, became a place Abbey went to eat, sleep and study.

Sighing, Abbey turned to face the barn. It once had been a grand structure. There were thirty cow stanchions, stalls for six teams of horses and farrowing crates for twenty sows.

Her father had never milked over ten cows, had never owned a team of horses, had never raised hogs.

Some men weren't meant to be farmers. Her father had been one of them.

The loft was immense. It had been a great place to play in inclement weather. She and Travis had mounted a basketball hoop at one end of the loft. They'd practiced dribbling the ball and shooting—

He kept slipping into her thoughts. No warning, just gliding in, taking over. But there was no harm done, she assured herself. Travis didn't know she was thinking about him.

She headed for the shed, blinded by tears. She wasn't crying for herself and Travis. Her tears for them had been surrendered years ago. She cried for the barn. There was no saving it. It was leaning, propped on the outside with heavy beams.

All it needed to come tumbling down was a nudge in the right place. She was surprised Travis hadn't done it.

Travis abruptly shoved aside the papers he'd been working on. His neck was aching. He'd bent over the desk too long. He rubbed the back of his neck. The muscles were tight, his skin hot—dammit! Wherever Abbey was, she was thinking of him! There wasn't leeway for doubt. He knew it with the same surety that he knew his name.

Was she sticking him with mental pins?

He started to stand but willed himself to stay put. He wasn't going to try to find her. He was crazy to even be thinking about her, thinking back to when she'd been his best friend, because she'd also been his worst enemy.

Loving her hadn't been easy. She'd ripped him apart. The best thing she'd ever done for him was to walk out of his life.

If she had been pregnant, if they had married, they'd have made each other miserable.

So why did he want to see her? To prove to himself that he was content with himself, with his life? To prove that he didn't feel anything special for Abbey? That the connectedness he'd thought he'd felt was an illusion?

Even if it was real, he never experienced that kind of thing with the woman he'd been dating. Hilary. He stared out the window. Hilary was blond and... For crying out loud, he didn't know the color of her eyes. Come to think of it, he didn't know much more about Hilary other than she was a teacher... easy to be with....

Wait a minute, he told himself. It would come to him. He'd looked into Hilary's eyes. He knew she had... blue eyes. Yes! Blue.

Maybe.

He rubbed his neck again, closed his eyes. Tension, he told himself. Tension spelled Abbey. The picture of a young Abbey formed against his eyelids. She was sitting in the bromegrass next to the creek, bent, tying her shoes. Her golden-brown braids, tied with red ribbons, swung over her shoulder. When she looked up her brown eyes were laughing.

Where was she if she wasn't at Cassie's? The farm! Of course! The Penny place.

He mumbled a profanity in annoyance with himself. He'd lost her a long time ago. He was *not* going through the pain of losing her again.

He had to convince her to give up, get out of his life.

It was on the way to the shed that Abbey first noted the yard had been mowed and the flower beds weeded. The early irises were blooming in masses of yellow and pale blue. It seemed an incongruity that care had been given the yard and not the buildings. Then again she'd learned Travis's strong suit was not reliability.

She opened the door of the shed to a clutter of furniture and stacks of boxes. Three of the walls were lined with rough shelving. They were filled with more boxes.

Her Great-grandmother Penny's straight-backed Shaker rocker was sitting in a far corner. Bob and Cassie might want to use it, she thought. There was a library table with marble mosaic ornamentation, a Windsor arrow-back settee, several chests, plant stands and candle stands and a pedestal, sectional dining-room table, which had been her mother's favorite.

On her next trip she'd rent a van to take the dining-room table back to Minneapolis. Then all she would need was a china cabinet. And chairs, of course. She would have to buy chairs.

The table had once had four matching chairs and a captain's chair. Her father had sold the four chairs at a neighbor's auction in order to pay a small, but long overdue bill with the Feed Elevator. But before he got to the Feed Elevator, he stopped at Milt's Bar and Grill.

He'd have sold the captain's chair, too, but one rung had been broken. The chair was stored in the shed, the rung on one of the shelves. Her mother had kept the chair, saying her father would get around to mending it someday.

Even though Abbey had witnessed the relationship between her parents, she'd never understood it. Or more accurately, she'd never understood why her mother stayed with her father.

Of course, there had been times when he was loving. But more times when his drinking made him sullen, filled with self-pity.

Taking care not to rub against anything, Abbey worked her way to the shelves where she believed the boxes holding the bone china were stored. She pulled a box from the shelf, set it on the library table and dusted off the lid before opening it.

The box contained twelve cups and twelve saucers, each piece wrapped separately in newspaper. The paper was yellowed and brittle. She closed the lid and set the box aside.

Working quickly, she checked four more boxes, all holding china. She reached for a fifth and smaller box. The moment she saw her mother's writing, Handle with Care, she knew what was inside. A vegetable bowl, cleanly broken in two pieces.

Her father had felt badly about allowing the bowl to slip through his fingers when her mother had passed it to him. He hadn't intended to fumble it, no more than he'd intended to have more than one drink at Milt's, no more than he'd intended to forget the hour, so that by the time he arrived home the chores and milking were done and dinner was cold.

Abbey knew her father had given her mother the dishes as a gift the first year they were married, so Abbey had expected the bowl to be mended. Her mother had never done it. When Abbey asked about it, her mother had told her that once something was broken, no matter how hard you tried to patch it, it was never as strong as it was in the beginning.

And still she'd saved the pieces.

Had her mother been talking about mending the bowl? Abbey wondered. Or had she been talking about her efforts to mend a broken marriage?

She started to lift the box back to the shelf—and smelled the scent of his cologne before his hands slid over hers.

"Where do you want it? The top shelf?" Travis asked, taking the box from her.

Abbey, hand over her heart, spun free from the accidental embrace. "Yes. Top shelf," she said.

He placed the box on the shelf and turned toward her, reaching for the hand she was holding over her heart. He held it while he studied her. "I didn't mean to frighten you," he said.

He had frightened her, she assured herself. She'd been concentrating. And he'd surprised her. That was why she was trembling. *Don't let it be because he's touching me.*

"You gave me a shock, but I'm okay," she said. He dropped her hand but continued to examine her. "Do I have dirt on my face?" she asked, laughing nervously.

"Dust," Travis said. He reached with his free hand to brush her right cheek.

The only times Abbey could recall responding to a dark look were when the look had come from Travis. And it had sparked passion. That was what she saw in his eyes now—passion.

For one, stupefying moment she found herself thinking it didn't matter that he'd hurt her, it didn't matter that he planned to hurt her again. She wanted to whisper, *Hold me, Travis. Hold me.*

She hardened her thoughts. Long ago she'd determined she would never make love again with a man who didn't love her. Travis hadn't loved her then. He didn't love her now.

She slipped her hand from his and edged away. "What are you doing here?" she asked, making sure she didn't sound shaken.

"Cassie called the office, thinking she might catch you," he said. "She wanted to make sure you showed for lunch. Jill's back for the weekend."

"That's wonderful! I haven't seen Jill in such a long time," Abbey said. "I was just finishing up here. I'm heading to town."

"Finishing up? Doing what?" Travis asked.

"I was refreshing my memory on what furniture was stored here, because Cassie and Bob might want to use some of it," Abbey said, sounding rushed. He'd delivered the message. Why didn't he leave? "I'll come back after I've changed clothes to load Mother's china—"

"The white bone?" Travis asked.

He did remember. So what? "I thought I'd take the dishes back with me this trip."

"I wouldn't have razed the shed without removing your things and storing them somewhere else," he said, sounding defensive.

"Did I imply that I thought you would?"

"You were thinking it."

"The thought that you might send a bulldozer rumbling over this shed *never* crossed my mind, because I have not given up on buying the buildings," Abbey snapped.

"Do give it up, Abbey. You'll only get hurt if you don't."

His closeness was a distraction. She heeded his warning but not the way he'd meant. He could hurt her. There was some mystical link to him that she hadn't severed. And that angered her.

"I'm amazed that you're so concerned about me," she said.

Sighing, Travis turned in the doorway and looked out, surveying the farmstead. He needed a distraction. When he'd touched her with no warning, he'd needed her. The physical attraction was there. Undeniably there. But the greater threat was the trap he'd always fallen into with Abbey. She involved him emotionally. And now he was aware that he'd been emotionally deprived in his relationships with other women. Or he had deprived them of his full attention.

Maybe it was because Abbey had been the only one who'd caused him to despair. Maybe it was because she was also the only one who'd ever given him an emotional high.

"What are you thinking?" she asked.

Travis glanced over his shoulder, didn't like what he saw in Abbey's expression and looked back to the yard. He had hired a man to do the yard work, asking that he pay particular attention to the perennial flower beds Jen had maintained.

"I'm thinking about transplanting some of the perennials at my house. The mums, asters—"

"You're the one who's been doing the yard work?"

"I hire someone."

"Why?"

"Some of the flowers are as old as the house," he said. "And they're worth saving."

"So is the house."

Besides the flowers, there was nothing here to salvage, Travis thought. Couldn't she see that? He didn't know why he was trying to talk sense into her. She never listened. He turned to face her and found defiance still in her eyes, in the set lines of her lips.

Why was it, he reflected, that words he spoke in trying to soothe her, stoked anger? His demonstrations of affection ended in disaster.

"I wish for your sake they were worth saving," he stated. "I'm not trying to hurt you."

"Maybe not, but you are and you know you are," she said. "And you're still going to do what you want to do."

"*We*'ve hurt each other," he said sharply. "We have always hurt each other. Why do we do it?"

She looked past him, out the door, obviously wishing he'd leave. "I don't know," she said. "But maybe an old adage applies."

"Which old saying?"

Her gaze was piercing when it came to him. "The one that says familiarity breeds contempt."

"Contempt?" he asked. "Contempt on whose part?"

"Yours," she said calmly. But her breasts moved with her rapid breathing.

His reaction was startling. His need for her grew until it was like a physical hunger.

"Never contempt," he said slowly.

"It seemed like contempt to me," she said.

"You make me sound ruthless at eighteen," he said.

"You thought I was ruthless also, didn't you?" she asked.

The question was colored with curiosity and an ounce of needling. "I didn't think you were ruthless." He leaned on the doorjamb, crossed his arms. "I thought you were inflexible."

The low vibrations of his voice caused a stirring in Abbey's chest. And the way he was leaning casually on the doorjamb, smiling lazily, gave her ample opportunity to observe his masculinity. She *was* physically attracted to him.

In an effort to extinguish the sparks shooting throughout her body, she said, "Maybe I was inflexible, but you were closed-minded. Maybe that's why we could never talk things through."

"You told me that I was the only one you could talk to," he countered.

"You were," Abbey admitted. "I relied on you. But I should have known better, because that's the same mistake Mother made with my father. She relied solely on him. He used her. And I ended up feeling used by you."

Abbey saw Travis thinking furious thoughts. She feared hearing them. "I'm sorry, Travis," she said quickly. "That was unfair of me. I know no one can be used unless they're willing to be used. I really don't want to fight with you."

"We aren't fighting," he said icily.

"Did you hear the tone of your voice?" Abbey asked. "If we keep talking about the past, we'll fight. You know it."

"You still blame me—"

"Please! Let's drop it," Abbey pleaded. "I want to go to Bob and Cassie's."

Abbey had expected an argument from Travis. He didn't give her one. Instead he left abruptly, walking in long, brisk strides toward his pickup.

Feeling as if she'd escaped from a ticking time bomb, Abbey closed the shed door. She was glad he'd given up without a fight. There were enough problems to deal with in the present without dredging up the past.

With luck she wouldn't have to see him again. With luck she could work through Roy. Yet when she turned to see that he was standing by his pickup waiting for her, she couldn't convince herself she was unlucky.

"You're right," he said as she walked toward him. "There's nothing to be gained by rehashing the problems we had."

"I couldn't agree more," she said.

"Cassie invited me to lunch," he said.

"She did?" Abbey asked, dumbfounded.

"Surprised?"

"Well...yes."

"She broke the rules, didn't she?" he asked.

"What rules?" Abbey asked.

"I'll put it in plain English," Travis said. "I've never told Bob or Cassie not to invite me when they knew you were going to be there. Have you ever said, 'Don't invite me if you're inviting Travis'?"

"Never," Abbey said.

"But because they're our friends, they knew we didn't want to be together. Right?"

"Yes," Abbey said. "I agree that you're right."

"I gathered from Cassie that they're fed up with being caught in the middle."

"I see," Abbey said.

"I'm wondering if the time hasn't come to ease up on them. Would you object if I were to come to lunch?"

Object? Abbey thought. She could list a hundred reasons why she should object. She also knew Travis was right. She'd known for a long time how their friends felt about getting trapped in the middle.

"Of course not," she said.

"I have to stop at the pit to check on a broken auger," he said. "Tell Cassie I'll be there for lunch, will you?"

"Sure," Abbey said. "I'll tell her."

Only after Travis's pickup was kicking up dust in the lane did Abbey wonder how, after ten years of diligently avoiding mentioning his name, she was going to casually offer that he was coming to lunch.

For sure she would have to do something about the bizarre beating of her heart, the warmth in her cheeks.

Had she missed Travis so much that even the prospect of arguing with him was preferable to not seeing him again?

Abbey didn't have time to sort through her emotions during the short drive to the Dillers' acreage on the north edge of town. She parked by the garage.

The house Bob and Cassie had remodeled was a Victorian structure. It contained eight rooms on two stories. It was shaded by huge, old trees, yet enough sunlight reached the windows to make them shimmer, giving the house a warm, welcoming appearance.

Jill and Cassie flew through the front door. A moment later Abbey was hauled from her car and mauled by enthusiastic embraces.

"Long time, no see and all that kind of stuff," Jill said. She hugged Abbey hard.

"I'm so glad you're here," Abbey said.

Jill was the shortest of the three friends. Green-eyed and petite, she had explosive energy. She wore clothes in daring color combinations, but managed to appear trend-setting rather than eccentric. Today her flowered blouse was bold both in color and pattern, but her jeans were plain and the waist sash an uninspired bone white.

"The way you're looking at me, I just know you haven't outgrown your urge to offer constructive comments about what I'm wearing," Jill said. "Have at it, but no teasing that my mother must have had a love affair with a house painter."

Abbey laughed. "I've never said that. Never even implied it."

"Bob was the one who said it," Cassie offered gleefully.

"My cousin never had taste," Jill retorted, rushing to add when Cassie frowned, "except in women. In women—whoops—woman, he has exemplary taste."

Cassie smiled. Jill turned back to Abbey. "What do you think of my blouse?"

"It's eye-catching. But you're getting conservative, aren't you?" Abbey asked. "No plaid or polka-dot pants."

Jill smiled complacently. "I forgot to pack my purple plaid knee-knockers."

"Purple is good," Abbey said, keeping a straight face.

"Listen," Cassie said, "I don't want to act bored with all the talk about clothes, but I am. Where have you been, Abbey?"

Cassie had had her dark hair cut and permed since Abbey had seen her last. She was the tallest of the three, standing five foot nine to Abbey's five foot eight. She never dieted, was naturally slender.

When they were younger, Travis had teased Cassie about looking lean and hungry. Abbey wondered if, when she wasn't around, he still teased Cassie and still picked up Jill as easily as if she were a feather duster.

"You were worried about me?" Abbey asked. "I'm flattered."

"Answer the question," Cassie said.

"Okay. Okay," Abbey said. "After seeing Travis at his office, I stopped at the farm, checked to see what was in the shed. Travis found me there."

His name had slipped out naturally. Her friends' stunned silence was unnatural. "You did send Travis to find me, didn't you?"

"No," Cassie said. "I didn't."

If Cassie hadn't asked Travis to find her, why had he come to the Penny place?

The realization struck her like a fist to the jaw, staggering and hurting. He'd tracked her down to argue her out of pursuing buying the buildings... talking to his dad.

But she hadn't given him the chance, and that was why he'd decided to come to lunch—to try to find a way to get her to give up.

All that talk about their friends feeling caught in the middle had been a ruse. Ten years hadn't mellowed him. He still had to have everything his own way.

## Chapter Four

Abbey reached into the back seat and lifted her overnight case from the car, then shut the door. "Travis asked me to tell you he'd decided to come to lunch."

"He did? Mind if I ask what happened?" Cassie asked.

They started up the walk. "Pretty much what I expected," Abbey said. "Travis refused to discuss selling the buildings. He's set on razing them."

Jill bounced up the porch steps to open the door. As Abbey and Cassie passed through into the entry hall, she observed, "If Travis is coming for lunch, he must believe the two of you can reach some kind of agreement about the Penny place."

"What he thinks is that he can persuade me to forget it."

"Did he say why he's razing the buildings?" Jill asked.

"In his opinion they're a hazard," Abbey said. "I've asked him to hold off razing until I've had the chance to try to contact Roy."

"I can just imagine how Travis reacted to that," Jill said. "At least, I know how I'd feel if someone tried to undermine my authority."

Abbey hadn't thought of it as undermining Travis's authority. "Whose side are you on?" she asked, only half teasing.

"Nobody's side," Jill said seriously. "But we aren't having a class election where the three of us automatically outvote Bob and Travis."

"Let's drop the subject before the two of you really get into it," Cassie said. She led the way down the hall toward the stairs. "We'll get you settled first, Abbey. Later we'll tour the house."

Abbey glanced into the front room as she followed Cassie and Jill to the stairs. An old, refinished oak organ sitting close to the fireplace was the focal point of the room, complemented by comfortable furniture.

"I think you'll be interested in some of the pieces in the shed," she said when she joined her friends on the stairs. "Shall we run out and take a look after lunch?"

"I can't," Cassie said forlornly. "They called from the lab this morning, apologized for calling while I was on vacation, but half the staff is fighting spring colds. I'm going in for an abbreviated shift, two until seven. How about tomorrow morning after church?"

"Good enough," Abbey said.

"I promised my parents I'd go with them to Sioux City to look for a whirlpool. Want to ride along?" Jill offered.

Abbey hesitated a moment. "I'd love to go, but I think I'd better start sorting through the shed. See exactly what is in all those boxes."

Cassie opened the guest bedroom door and settled on a settee, stretching her legs out in catlike contentment.

Jill plopped onto the bed, and Abbey put her suitcase on the other end. She never realized how she missed being with Cassie and Jill until she was with them.

She unlocked the suitcase. She hadn't brought much along. Changes of undergarments, nightgown. Blouses and jeans. She'd change before lunch. Had Travis really seen dust on her cheek and brushed it away? She raised her hand, touched her cheek where he'd touched her. How could he, through a touch, a look, make her believe she was beautiful.

"How's life treating you, Abbey?" Jill asked.

Abbey jerked to attention. She couldn't have a private thought with Cassie and Jill around. Which was probably a good thing, she decided. It wasn't the thoughts she uttered that got her in trouble, but the ones she privately contemplated. Like why she still loved Travis's touch when she didn't love him.

She lifted the blouses from the suitcase, set them aside to hang later, slipped the nightgown and undergarments into a dresser drawer.

"Can you be more specific than life?" she asked.

"Start with Evan. Are you still seeing him?" Jill asked. When Abbey nodded, she asked, "What has it been? Six, eight months?"

"Six," Abbey said.

"Fascinating," Jill observed. "He's lasted longer than anyone else you've dated."

Abbey shut the drawer. She carried the blouses to the closet to hang them. "I like him," she said, "but I'm not in love with him."

"Do what I've decided to do," Jill advised. "The first man I meet and like, I am deliberately going to fall in love with him."

"The Arizona sun has baked your brain," Cassie countered disdainfully. "You can deliberately work to improve your marriage, but you can't deliberately fall in love."

Jill shrugged. "I'm being realistic, Cassie. Romantic love is an illusion."

Cassie groaned. "Does that groan of condescension mean you see stars when Bob kisses you?"

Cassie's answer was a low chuckle, which caused Abbey to hesitate before she hung the last blouse. Apparently Cassie felt *something*. Something very special.

"You watch," Jill said. "The first man who sparks my curiosity and I'm off in hot pursuit."

"You're impossible," Cassie said. "She's impossible, isn't she, Abbey?"

Did it make sense to work on falling in love? Abbey wondered. "She's always been impossible," she said, smiling.

"Say!" Cassie exclaimed. "News flash! Tom Green is back."

"I'd heard from Meg that Tom was back," Abbey said as Jill blurted, "I thought Clara's husband was dead."

Abbey slid the jeans into a drawer, closed the suitcase and set it aside, then eased down onto the end of the bed. Cassie filled in the details of Tom Green's reappearance.

"It's hard to describe the tenderness they display toward one another," she concluded, "but it's truly awesome."

"Grandpa Fulbright said Clara and Tom were renting a farm next to them when Tom took off," Jill said. "He says he and Tom were pretty good friends, but Tom left without so much as a hint to him about what he was planning."

"Sixty years apart," Cassie pondered. "But they've obviously forgiven themselves and each other for the mistakes of the past."

The conversation drifted from the Greens to tidbits about what else was happening around town. Cassie stood, saying she had to get the steaks out for Bob to grill. Jill offered to toss the salad and when Cassie accepted, she eased from the bed.

After Cassie and Jill left, Abbey slowly slipped from her suit jacket, carrying it to the closet to hang it. Had she forgiven herself for being too dependent on Travis? For being too trusting?

Her thoughts jumped to Evan. He *had* lasted longer than any other man she'd dated, but recently she had begun to find fault with him. She'd been irritated when he'd assumed they had a date last night.

Was she about to do to him what she'd done to other men she'd dated, draw away rather than work to cement the relationship?

Was forgiving herself for being too dependent, too trusting with Travis the key to forging a meaningful relationship with Evan?

At the moment she didn't have time to ponder the possibilities with Evan. At the moment there was the Penny place. What she could do and couldn't do with Travis.

Abbey washed up, changed into stone-washed jeans with decorator brass buttons and slipped into a simple white blouse with buttons that matched the ones on the jeans. Then she hurried to join Cassie and Jill.

When she got to the kitchen, Abbey saw Bob had arrived and had already started the steaks. She stepped outside to visit with him a minute, then went back to the kitchen to see whether she could help.

Cassie handed her a tray with dishes and silverware to set the patio table. She had just put down the dishes and silverware when Travis's black pickup swung into the driveway.

Abbey reaffirmed in her mind that her first priority wasn't to wandering down the pathways of the past. She was here to save the farmstead. Just as Travis's priority was trying to convince her she had no right to oppose him.

She didn't begrudge him that, but it steamed her to think he'd used their friends to try to gain his objective. And the more she thought about it, the more steamed she became.

Yet her undisciplined heart skipped a beat when Cassie stepped from the kitchen onto the patio, saying, "Travis is here, Bob. Are the steaks done?"

"I saw him drive in." Bob tested a steak with the tine of the long-handled fork. "Medium rare all around. Won't be long."

Cassie set the bowls of food she was carrying on the table, walked to Bob and brushed his cheek with a kiss, murmuring something that made him chuckle.

Jill carried two pitchers of iced tea from the kitchen, set them on the table, then went to greet Travis.

"Hello, stranger," she said.

Travis scooped Jill into his arms and swung her around. "What's my favorite social worker been doing lately?" he asked. "Chasing men too old to outrun you?"

"That deserves no answer." Jill pounded his shoulders. "Put me down, Travis!"

There was laughter in Travis's voice, in his smile, Abbey reflected. He was truly happy to see Jill. But the smile vanished when he set Jill on the ground and looked over her head to where Abbey was standing.

So he wasn't overjoyed to see her. She didn't care, but if he'd been the least bit sincere about easing the tension between them for the sake of their friends, he could have pretended a smile for her.

As she was pretending a smile for him. "Hello, Travis," she said.

"Hello, Abbey."

Travis's gaze stayed on Abbey, when she turned away to finish placing silverware by each plate. What had he expected by way of greeting? he wondered. That she'd rush into his arms? No. He hadn't expected that, but when they'd parted, he'd believed she was going to be cordial.

Yet the moment their gazes met over Jill's head, he'd known she wasn't welcoming him but merely tolerating his presence.

"So I have plenty of time to do all the things I want to do," Jill was saying.

When Travis realized his gaze had lingered on Abbey, he forced it back to Jill. "That's nice," he said.

"You really think so?" Jill asked.

Her eyes were sparkling devilishly. She'd trapped him and Travis knew it. He laughed. "Got me. What did you say?"

"You asked what I'd been doing," Jill said. "I blatantly lied, telling you that I'd been fired. It's showing, Travis."

"What's showing?" Travis asked, knowing exactly what Jill meant.

"The itch you still have for Abbey."

"That's bluntly put," Travis said, trying to pass off the accuracy of her observation with lightheartedness. "When did you stop being a lady?"

"I've always called it like I saw it," Jill retorted. "Going to do anything about the itch?"

"Nope," Travis said firmly. "Abbey and I still rub each other the wrong way."

"Resulting in friction," Jill said.

"Definitely."

"Friction is the result of chemistry," Jill observed. "Can't have friction unless the chemistry is right."

"True. But create enough friction and you create a breakdown."

"Without friction," Jill countered, "you couldn't drive or stop a car. The breeze wouldn't rustle the leaves on the trees. And most important, without friction, a relationship could be summed up in one word—boring."

"Too much friction burns out a relationship," Travis countered.

"Soothing words keep it lubricated and get it over the rough spots."

"You're getting esoteric in your old age," Travis teased.

"And you, my friend, are just getting older." She laughed up at him.

"Come on, Travis and Jill," Cassie called. "You can't stand there visiting while the rest of us work. Travis, there's a bucket of ice in the freezer. Jill, get the cake, will you?"

Travis called back, "Why are you ordering me and asking Jill?"

"Don't be a sorehead," Cassie said. "Just do it."

When he and Jill came back with the ice and cake and it came to sitting down, Travis noted that Abbey was waiting to see where he was going to sit. When he sat down next to Jill, she slid between Bob and Cassie.

She was directly opposite him. She'd washed off her makeup and was hauntingly beautiful without it. In her jeans and blouse, her hair loose, she looked like the old Abbey, which was a tormenting thought.

The conversation picked up and continued nonstop through the lunch of rib eyes, crisp salad and buns fresh from the oven. Once the dishes had been cleared, they lounged on patio chairs, drinking coffee before

Bob went back to the store, Jill left to go with her parents and Cassie left for her shift at the hospital.

Travis didn't add much to the conversation. He listened and waited for Abbey to say something, anything to him. She had already sidestepped him several times when he tried to engage her in conversation.

"I hate to run off and leave you, Abbey," Cassie said.

"No problem. It will take me several hours to sort through the shed."

"Wait until tomorrow morning and we'll help, when we're getting what Cassie wants to use," Bob offered.

"I think that might rush me," Abbey said. "I have to leave by noon."

"What's the rush?" Bob asked.

"No rush," Abbey said. "But I have the weekend routine to catch up when I get back. Laundry. Hair. Fun things like that."

Travis drained his coffee. Didn't that sound familiar, he thought. For Abbey, time in Beaver Crossing had always been measured in how many months, days and hours she had to spend before she could leave.

Abbey glanced at him, her lips set in straight lines. She looked back at Bob and smiled.

Didn't their friends notice how Abbey's smile passed over him? Travis wondered. How her laughter was only sincere when the cause of it wasn't him? Suddenly he was irked. At her. At himself.

Abbey forced herself to listen as Bob described the improvements he'd made at the store—new checkout counters, new upright freezers. And she wanted to care about what he was doing, but she didn't.

And she wanted to care about the administrative position Jill had been offered at a senior citizens' center, but she couldn't. She only cared about how Travis was treating her.

Didn't anyone but Travis and herself feel the tension?

No, she thought. Cassie and Jill were talking in low tones, chuckling. Travis's gaze was on them.

She laughed when Bob told a joke, even though she'd missed the punch line. Travis's gaze met hers, darkening. She looked away.

She knew what he was thinking. In spite of her, he was going to raze the buildings. They were in the way of something he wanted. And he was determined to prune them out.

Just as he'd pruned her out of his life, as if she was so much deadwood.

But it wasn't going to happen this time. This time she wasn't going to let him push her out of his way.

# Chapter Five

"**I** don't know whether I actually remember it or have been reminded of that day so often that I think I remember it," Cassie said.

"Remember what?" Bob asked.

"Cassie and I were talking about our first day of school," Jill said. She pulled her legs up, curled them to the side. "Cassie thinks we were too young to remember it. But I do."

"How could you forget?" Travis asked, grinning. "You were sprawled in the hallway outside the classroom, kicking and hanging onto your mother's ankles, bawling, 'Don't leave me, Ma. Don't leave me.'"

"It wasn't that bad," Jill countered, laughing.

"Oh yes, it was that bad," Abbey said.

"Look who's talking," Jill said. "I wasn't the only unhappy child that day."

Abbey had never spent more than a couple of hours away from her mother, never had a playmate other than Travis. Despite her mother's attempts to assure her that going to school would be fun, the idea of riding the huge, yellow bus and meeting a bunch of children she didn't know had been frightening.

"I was a little scared," she said, smiling.

"Scared doesn't begin to describe it," Travis said. "I remember dragging you from the bus, up the sidewalk and into the schoolhouse."

Abbey joined in the laughter. Travis had kept telling her, "Come on, Abbey. Ain't nothing to be scared of, 'cause I'm your friend and I ain't goin' to let anybody hurt you."

Those had been his words. They were no figment of her imagination. And he hadn't allowed anyone to hurt her when they were six. He'd saved it until she loved him, and done it with words like, "Then I guess I'm not obligated to you anymore."

What had made him feel obligated to her in the first place? Who had designated him her protector? She'd proved she could survive without him. She'd have survived the first day of school without him, though in retrospect, it wouldn't have been as much fun.

"You're right," she admitted. "I was feeling vulnerable, and seeing Jill's demonstration of insecurity didn't mitigate my own."

"I'm truly contrite," Jill said.

"I can see that you are. Just about as contrite as you were when you bit Miss Fuller's finger," Abbey said.

"I nipped her finger!" Jill yelped.

"She screamed! You bit her," Cassie stated.

"She cussed, too," Bob observed. He laughed. "It was the first time I'd ever heard an adult say damn."

"With all the kicking and screaming and cussing going on," Abbey said, straight-faced, "no wonder I decided school wasn't the place for me."

"It broke loose then, didn't it?" Bob observed with a laugh. His laughter triggered a tickling ripple, touching everyone. Abbey laughed until tears formed in her eyes. She wiped them away.

She'd started to run down the hall. Travis had tackled her. Literally. Then he'd sat on her. Miss Burton, the first-grade teacher, had come from her room because of the commotion. She'd grabbed Travis by the shirt and pulled him from Abbey's back, then held him.

When Abbey had seen what appeared to be a threat to Travis, she'd forgotten her own fear and tried to rescue Travis. She'd clamped onto Travis's pants, while Miss Burton retained possession of his shirt. What had resulted was a tug-of-war.

Cassie and Bob, who had been silent observers to that point, decided to leave. It had taken Jill's mother, Miss Fuller, Miss Burton and the principal an hour to round up, reestablish order and settle the five of them in for their first day of school. The smallest class in the history of Beaver Crossing had made itself known.

Cassie, hiccuping, said, "I . . . think that first day is when the teachers labeled us habitual troublemakers."

Genuine emotion had softened Travis's lips. When he smiled as he was smiling, she always wanted to kiss him. Always? Like a habit? Abbey pondered. Had

Travis been a habit with her? Had she used him as a crutch because he made her feel secure?

Jill glanced at her watch. "It's been fun, but I've got to run. Are we still planning on meeting for dinner at Irene's Café?"

Earlier Bob had suggested they meet for dinner there. Travis hadn't responded one way or another. Nor had Abbey.

She wasn't sure she wanted to be with Travis at Irene's. Being around him was difficult enough, without returning to the spot where they'd parted so bitterly that hot, August afternoon ten years ago. She wished there were some way to wiggle out of going, without appearing to be wiggling.

"That's okay with you, isn't it, Abbey?" Cassie asked. "If we eat around nine?"

Abbey looked up. Good grief. There was no wiggle room in answering a direct question. "Oh. Sure," she said. "Fine with me."

"How about you?" Bob asked Travis.

"I don't know—"

"Already have plans?" Bob interrupted.

Abbey pretended she hadn't heard Bob ask, but she thought she could hear Travis breathing as she waited for his answer. Was he still going with the lawyer? Evelyn something or other? Maybe they were engaged?

"Tentative plans," Travis said. "Nothing binding. If I'm not at Irene's by nine, I won't be there."

Cassie grabbed the glasses and headed into the house to get ready for work. Bob and Travis walked toward their pickups, while Jill and Abbey walked to their cars.

"I think it went okay, don't you?" Jill asked.

"The meal was great."

"I was talking about you and Travis," Jill said. "You didn't cross swords once, even though it was a bit tense."

"You noticed?" Abbey asked.

"You could cut it with a knife, as the saying goes," Jill said. "But it will be better the next time."

"I doubt if there will be a next time," Abbey said.

"Oh, there will be."

"I don't think he intends to meet us at Irene's tonight," Abbey said. "Is he still going with the lawyer?"

"Lawyer?" Jill said. "Oh, you mean Evelyn."

"Evelyn."

Jill stopped, dug in her jeans pocket and came out with the key to her parents' car. "Thank goodness. For a minute I thought I'd lost it." Her gaze came to Abbey. "What was the question?"

"No question," Abbey said. She started to her car.

"Cassie says he's been going with someone called Hilary. I've never met her. I did meet Joan. Didn't like her much, but I did like Mary Ann. And Marcella was nice."

For heaven's sake, Abbey thought. She could count on the fingers of one hand, minus two fingers, the men she'd dated.

"He's been busy, hasn't he," Abbey said.

"That's something else I've decided," Jill said, stepping to the car and opening the door. "If Travis can have a bachelor pad, I ought to be able to have a bachelorette pad. I'm going to start swinging."

Abbey laughed. "You?"

"I can dream, can't I?"

"Come on, Jill," Abbey said. "You're making me nervous. If I didn't know you, I'd think you were serious about finding a 'suitable' man and working to fall in love with him."

Jill studied Abbey. "Instead of serious, you wanted to say desperate, didn't you?"

"Yes," Abbey said. "And I know you aren't desperate. You have a good job, the offer of a better one—"

"Stop right there," Jill interrupted. "Sometimes I feel all I've done with my life is work to get ahead in my profession."

"You can't tell me you haven't wanted to do exactly that," Abbey said. "Or that your work hasn't made you happy."

"It makes me happy," Jill agreed. "Then I come home, witness the significant relationship between my parents and have this vision of growing old alone. I don't mind telling you it scares me."

"Being married isn't the answer for everyone," Abbey said. "It wasn't for my parents."

"I can't argue with that," Jill said. "But I know positively that I want to take a chance on coupleness." She climbed into the car, closed the door. "See you later."

Coupleness, Abbey thought. Coupleness?

Travis drove away slowly, looking into his rearview mirror to where Jill and Abbey were standing, engaged in conversation.

The tension between Abbey and himself had been broken briefly when they laughed about the first day of school. Abbey's face had glowed. But she'd flinched when the subject of meeting at Irene's came up. He'd flinched, too.

The memory of the day he'd waited in his pickup for Abbey to get off work rose up to scorch him. He'd hoped they could work something out, but one bitter word had led to another and when she'd slammed the door as she left, he'd known it was over.

He wouldn't go tonight. He knew it would be more comfortable for Abbey if he didn't. What was left was the business with the Penny place. What Abbey wanted as opposed to what he wanted, emotions left out of it.

He turned down the lane to the Penny place, parked his pickup in back of the house and waited for Abbey to show.

She wasn't long in coming.

Abbey wasn't surprised to see Travis waiting for her. He hadn't had the opportunity to "work" on her during lunch. She stopped by the shed, popped the trunk lid, then stepped from the car.

"We need to talk," he said when he joined her.

She opened the shed. "Sure," she said. "We can talk while I sort."

"Should I back up the pickup?" he asked.

"What for?"

"Thought maybe you want something taken to the landfill."

Abbey stepped into the shed. "I'm only going to load the dishes, look through the boxes stored on the shelves." She turned to face him. "You can't talk me out of talking to your dad or trying to buy the buildings."

"Dammit, Abbey—"

"I know it looks as if I'm trying to undercut your authority—"

"Looks like?" Travis countered. "It is undercutting it."

"That really is not my intention," Abbey said. "I want to hear what Roy has to say."

"All right. But before you call him, come with me to take a close look at the buildings. Let me point out what the architect pointed out to me," Travis said.

"I doubt that I'll have time today," she said. "I want to visit Clara."

"I'll wait," Travis said. He leaned against the wall, folded his arms. "You might change your mind."

Great, Abbey thought. Bad enough that he was here. Worse having him look over her shoulder while she worked. "Wait if you want to wait, but this is going to take a while."

"Fine," he said.

Abbey nodded. She'd ignore him.

She took a box from the shelf, set it on the library table and opened it. It contained scrap material. As did a second and third box. She recognized a red cotton fabric her mother had used in sewing a dress for Mrs. Ames, a blue satin used in the dress Mrs. Noble had made for her daughter's wedding.

The fabrics were musty-smelling, had been chewed by mice for nesting. When she cleared out the shed, the boxes would have to be thrown away.

She could feel Travis watching her. She didn't want him to talk to her, but his not saying a word, just watching and waiting, was getting on her nerves.

But if it was a nerve game they were playing, she would take her sweet time looking through the boxes. He'd get bored and leave.

She opened another box, expecting to find more material, but it was filled with the discarded pots, pans, bent silverware and the crock bowl she'd used when the shed had been her playhouse.

She forgot she was ignoring Travis.

"I'm beginning to think Mother didn't throw anything away." She lifted the crock and held it toward Travis. They couldn't have been more than eight when they'd run into trouble while making mud pies.

"You ready for the eggs now?" Travis asked.

"Yeah. I'm ready," she replied, falling easily into the same conversation they'd had on that calamitous day twenty years ago.

Travis pantomimed holding the two eggs they'd snatched from under one of her mother's brood hens. He frowned. "Does your mom know we're gonna use real eggs?"

"You're bossy," Abbey said. She set the crock on the table. "But this is my playhouse and so we'll do what I want to do. Crack 'em."

Grinning, Travis stepped forward. "Okay. Here goes." He pretended to whack the first egg on the edge of the bowl.

Abbey's laugh started as a cackle, grew until she doubled over. The egg had been rotten and had exploded like a bomb. They'd gagged and scrambled from the playhouse, gasping for fresh air. The playhouse had smelled like a skunk for a month.

As Travis laughed, he realized how much he'd missed Abbey's smile, her laughter; how it seemed to feed some hunger he hadn't known he'd had. Maybe it was part of the connectedness.

Suddenly his heartfelt desire was to forget the three turbulent months when sexuality had complicated their lives, ruined their friendship. He longed for the simpler time when they'd been innocent. When a kiss on the cheek was sublime.

"Hello, friend," he found himself saying. "You've been gone a long time. I've missed you."

Abbey looked into his eyes and wilted from the tenderness. Like a leaf blown before a brisk wind, she tumbled erratically back and forth between restraint and response. Then constraint vanished.

"Hello, friend," she said softly. She didn't shake him off when he placed his fingers under her forearms.

"I would very much like to kiss you," he murmured. He bent, brushed her cheek with his lips.

When his lips moved over her mouth, Abbey leaned back. "No more," she whispered.

"Why not?" he asked.

"There's no reason. It wouldn't be meaningful."

"Kissing you was always meaningful."

"Then it wouldn't be significant."

"Maybe I want to assure myself that kissing you wouldn't be significant," he countered.

Tom-toms beat in Abbey's temples. She was limp with anticipation. Weak from wanting him to stop teasing her with light caresses on her arms.

"Dammit," he groaned. "I've been telling myself I haven't missed kissing you." He pulled her toward him. "I want to see whether or not I've been lying to myself."

Her fingers splayed on his chest to push him away. The pads instantly flamed. She heard the voice of reason. She couldn't trust him. She couldn't trust herself. He was a nay-sayer. She was going to fight him.

Desperate to save herself from the embarrassment of having him realize he still had control over her physically, she said, "I'm thinking about getting married."

If she'd thought that would stop the drawing of their lips toward each other, stall the movement of their bodies toward each other, she was wrong.

"Do what you want to do, Abbey. You always have."

The words were breathed on her lips before his took possession of hers. She wanted to rail at him for hurling that admonition. But what she wanted more was to sink into the feel of him, to savor the sweet taste of him.

Her hands took flight, moving frantically over his body, the corded strength of his neck. She ran her fingers over the curve of his cheeks, where the skin was as smooth as she'd remembered, over the angle of his jaw where it was coarser.

She nibbled and flicked her tongue over his lower lip. She waited for her strength to drain away, but no weakness beset her. What she felt was more dangerous. She wanted to yield, open herself to him. Blend her soul with his.

And that couldn't be, she was thinking, when he deepened the kiss, dropped his hands to her buttocks, pressed her to him. Her lashes fell, not to shield her thoughts from him but in response to passion. Then it struck her.

This wasn't the young man who'd been as inexperienced as she when they'd made love. This was a man with expertise, gained through experience. Evelyn. Joan. Mary Ann. Hilary. Marcella. And she was just another experience.

She broke off the kiss, leaned back in his arms, her emotions fermenting. What did she say? You kiss terrifically?

My God, Travis thought in wonderment. What had made him think he could kiss her and walk away? He dropped his hands, eased away.

"I'd be lying if I didn't admit that kissing you is still significant," he said.

"I...remembered you as being a...less self-assured," Abbey stammered.

"Less self-assured?" he asked with a trace of humor.

"Ah...with less experience."

Travis was fighting for his life, torn between indolence and passion, mercilessness and tenderness, between acrimony and love.

"When we were making love I *was* inexperienced, Abbey. You didn't have the corner on virginity."

Abbey could have played shocked. She could have played indignant. But she was too hurt. Her sexual experience with men was limited. Very limited. Exclusively with him.

He wasn't taunting her. He'd simply answered the question she'd put to him. There was no logical thought behind what she was feeling, nothing to neatly wrap up why she should feel he owed her fidelity. But she did. And she felt he'd betrayed her.

She stuffed the crock bowl back into the box.

"Are you going to throw that box away?" Travis asked.

"I don't know," Abbey answered vaguely.

"Maybe you'll save it," he suggested quietly. "Your children might like to play with it someday."

"I doubt it," Abbey said. "Children play with plastic toys and video games today, not discarded pots and pans."

"Maybe they should," Travis said.

An errant thought flew through her mind. If she were to follow Jill's advice and deliberately fall in love with Evan, what kinds of toys would their children entertain themselves with?

No matter how hard she tried, she couldn't envision a child of Evan being satisfied playing with a box of junk. A child of Travis she could. A dark-haired, blue-eyed little boy, who would carry garter snakes and pretty-colored pebbles in his pocket.

That was what she missed, she suddenly realized. How she and Travis had been as children. It didn't explain all she was feeling, but she thought it was enough.

When she lifted the first box of dishes from the shelf, Travis took it from her. They worked in silence while loading the dishes into the trunk, Abbey wondering when he would get around to the subject of the buildings.

She took the box holding the broken vegetable bowl from the shelf, and stood pondering what to do with it.

"Want that box in the trunk?" he asked.

"I don't know. It's a broken bowl." She opened the box and handed it to him.

"I think the bowl could be mended," he observed. "I wonder why your mother didn't do it?"

"I asked Mother about mending the bowl," Abbey said. She told Travis about the night the bowl had been broken, about the conversation she'd had with her mother. "I think she might have been talking about her marriage."

"Possibly," Travis agreed.

Abbey sighed. "Whether she was talking about the fruitlessness of mending a broken bowl or a broken marriage, she was right either way."

"What are you going to do with the bowl?" Travis asked.

"Put it back on the shelf. Throw it away later with the rest of the junk," Abbey said.

"You aren't even going to try to repair it?"

"It wouldn't hold water, let alone hot vegetables," Abbey said. She shrugged her shoulders. "It's a piece of china not worth restoring."

Travis gave Abbey a curious look. He closed the box and returned it to the shelf, then moved to stand in the doorway. "Are you done here?" he asked.

"Done," Abbey said. Here it comes, she thought. He's going to bring up looking at the buildings. "Thanks for the help. Now I'll have more time to visit Clara."

"I want you to look at the buildings," he said. "You'll still have time to see Clara."

Abbey wasn't going to argue with him. She was simply going to leave. She moved toward where he was standing in the doorway.

He didn't step aside. She paced in a tight circle between the library table and a plant stand.

"Oh, oh."

She shot him a look. "'Oh, oh'? What does that mean?"

"You're in your pacing mode and I'm in trouble," he observed casually.

Abbey stopped, confronted him. "I'll admit I *used* to pace. It was a bad habit. I broke it. I don't pace anymore. And you aren't in trouble, because I'm not angry with you."

"My mistake. What were you doing there?" he asked, making a little circling motion with his hand. "And who, if not me, are you angry with?"

The sun shone in his hair at that particular moment and reflected raven highlights. He'd always washed his hair every day with a piney-smelling shampoo. He still did. She'd smelled it this morning, inhaled the piney forest when he kissed her.

Nature was playing tricks on her, Abbey thought. He had no right to look so confident when her world was reeling out of control, and she didn't know whether she was reeling because he wanted to wrench the farmstead from her or because he'd kissed other women. Or because he'd kissed her, and she knew she'd be a long time forgetting it.

"I'm angry with myself, because you can still weaken my resolve with a wink and a grin," she said. "So I'm mentally circling you while I figure out how to parry, because I am not going to be outmaneuvered, Travis.''

She'd expected a sharp retort from him. Not low laughter, not movement toward her so quick that she couldn't avoid him. And not a short embrace with the words, ''God, Abbey, I *have* missed you.''

## Chapter Six

If the words, "I have missed you," hadn't kept ringing in her ears, Abbey might have said no to looking at the buildings. Instead she said, "All right, we'll do it," and knew she sounded happy.

Smiling, Travis stepped from the shed. Abbey followed, closing and securing the door. When she joined him, he asked, "Around the lilac bushes or through them?"

The row of lilac bushes separating the house from the outbuildings were approximately a hundred feet long. Without pruning, the bushes had grown thick from bottom to top. They presented a formidable barrier.

"I don't think I'm up to the challenge of crawling on my hands and knees to get through," she said. "Guess I'll opt for the long way around."

"Right," Travis said, smiling. "You're an executive now. Can't expect you to shove your way through a thicket. By the way, when I learned you'd been promoted to head fashion buyer for the Hesston chain, I was pleased."

Abbey was genuinely surprised. "You were pleased?"

"I couldn't resent it, knowing how much you wanted it," he said. "Tell me about your work."

They stopped, standing in the shade of a bur oak, one Abbey had been told had been planted by her Great-Grandfather Penny.

"Cassie and Bob must have filled you in. Or Jill," Abbey said.

"Broad strokes of the brush," Travis said. "Paint in the details. Tell me about the personalities of the people around you."

Because she saw that Travis was truly interested, Abbey told him about Daniel Hesston. About Nicole, who was working her way into Abbey's affection. She told him about the people in the profession. About those who were open and friendly; about those, who because of their snobbish cliquishness, she avoided.

She grew animated in describing what she actually did most days, and watched Travis vicariously enjoying her successes, sympathizing with her setbacks.

If anything about Evan bothered her, it was his vague, almost abstract interest in her work. When he asked her about her day and she told him, he looked as if he were listening, but she knew his thoughts were a million miles away, probably on a brokerage transaction.

"You sound as if the thing you like most about your work isn't what you call the 'unglamorous grind' but Daniel Hesston himself," Travis observed.

"I do like and admire Daniel. To the point where I can't seem to say no when he asks me to work overtime or attend an evening business meeting," Abbey found herself admitting.

"And you won't, because you want to please him," Travis observed.

"I suppose you're right. But it's beginning to get to me. I barely find time to sketch an idea of my own, let alone sample materials and sit down at the sewing machine."

"If you feel that strongly about it, tell Daniel Hesston how you feel," Travis said.

"I don't know if I could go that far," Abbey said. "Loyalty to the job means everything to Daniel."

"I doubt that he'd fire you," Travis stated. "I don't know the man, don't understand the garment business, but he obviously knows a quality employee when he sees one. You're quality."

Abbey didn't understand why he was complimenting her. She didn't want to believe it could be to soften her up. "Any reason for the compliment?" she asked.

"Was it a compliment? I thought I was making a statement based on common sense. You had a head start on your competition. Jen taught you to sew by the time you were five," Travis said. "You were designing and making your own clothes by the time you were twelve. And you've always had a gut instinct for knowing what would make people stop and take notice."

His laugh was low. "Or maybe I should have said that I always sat up and took notice of what you were wearing. I'll never forget the dress you made for our senior prom. Silky material. Three shades of blue, the top a dark blue-green."

Abbey considered herself lucky they'd stopped under the shade of the oak. Its canopy was massive, the shade underneath deep. Deep enough to keep Travis from seeing the warmth creeping into her cheeks.

Senior prom night. They'd slipped away from the dance, ridden around the countryside in his car, an old convertible. They'd parked. They'd kissed. He'd run his fingers along the neckline of the dress, whispering in her ear, "It's too daring, Abbey."

He'd asked her to marry him. She'd told him she couldn't, not yet. And then she'd invited his love-making. It had been magnificently innocent, beautifully moving.

"I spent months looking for sale material," she said, her voice sounding fluttery. "The dress cost me twelve dollars and eighty-five cents."

Travis couldn't get past the memory of the first time they'd made love. He'd marveled at the whiteness of her skin, the softness of her body, her eagerness to please him. But he hadn't intended to bring the memory back for himself, or wonder if she remembered.

What had she said? Yes. The dress cost twelve dollars and eighty-five cents. She'd always taken pride in stretching every penny she earned working for Irene.

He cleared his throat. "Are you still a tightwad?" he asked.

"Yes," she said. "I'm still a tightwad."

"Old habits are hard to break," Travis said, smiling.

"I was wondering earlier how much of my life had been habit," she said.

Travis was attuned to the language her body spoke. She hadn't returned his smile. Her body had stiffened. She was rejecting him.

"I gather you were thinking about us? Being a habit?"

"I was thinking about us living next to each other all those years. I do think we were habit, more than anything else, don't you?"

Loving her hadn't been a habit with him, Travis thought. But he could believe he'd been a habit with her. He'd been too available, easy to resort to in a crisis.

"You're probably right," he said brusquely. "By the way, I like the outfit you're wearing now better than I did the suit you had on this morning."

He walked away, heading for the west side of the house and the basement door. The logical place to begin was the basement. The Penny house had been built in an era where the basement was more like a cellar, a place to store jars of canned fruit and vegetables and put the wood-burning furnace. The only access to it was from the outside of the house.

"What was wrong with my blue suit?" she asked as she joined him.

He wished she wasn't walking so close, wished he hadn't kissed her and felt the connectedness again. "Nothing," he said.

Abbey knew *that* tone of voice. "Nothing—but what?"

"Nothing, but it isn't you," Travis said.

She had put on the suit this morning because she'd known he would notice what she was wearing. She'd stopped at Jake's because she'd known he would study her.

"The blue suit *is* me. It's professional-looking without making me appear stiff, cold," she said.

"That's your opinion," he said. "In my opinion you're more warm and beautiful wearing blue jeans and no makeup."

"Well," Abbey said, taken aback, "you've a right to your opinion."

Travis smiled, bent and opened the basement door. "A thank-you would have been nice."

"Thank you."

"You're welcome. I thought we'd start here," he said.

"I'd gathered as much," Abbey said.

He laughed, then started down the steps. Abbey moved to the entry, lingering there while looking down into the damp darkness. The steps squeaked under Travis's weight. Partway down, he stopped, turned back. "Watch it," he advised. "A couple of steps are missing."

"Have you heard any mice?"

"Mice?"

"Those furry little rodents that scamper away when you approach. Heard any scampering?"

"You're procrastinating, Abbey."

"No. I really don't like the basement. It was dug out of the rock, just like a cave. It's cold and damp. I've seen snakes down there. They feed on the mice."

"Thanks for the science lesson," Travis said. He reached up, grasped her hand.

The shadowy gloom below seemed to lighten in proportion to his increasing pressure on her hand as he urged her to come toward him. She took the first steps slowly. When they reached the basement, he dropped her hand and directed her attention to the sill plates and floor joists.

"You can see they're rotten," he said. "I understand they can't be replaced unless the house is jacked and a new foundation set. But jack up the house and the rock of the walls would likely become unstable."

"It would be a big project," Abbey conceded.

"Big is right," he said. "The subfloor has to be replaced. The water pipes are rusted. The plumbing is shot throughout the house."

She was about to tell him he'd made his point when he went to the steps, climbed past the first missing one and turned, his hand extended to help her.

Once outside the house, he closed the basement door, then headed for the back porch. Obviously he'd decided to be thorough, Abbey thought. What was perplexing was that she wasn't nearly as eager to head into town to see Clara as she should be.

As they walked through the kitchen, Travis mentioned the windows—all thirty-two of them—would have to be replaced. As they walked through the dining room and front room, he told her the inside of the entire house would have to be gutted, insulated and plasterboarded.

As they climbed the winding stairs to the second floor, Abbey asked, "Did you get an estimate on the cost of restoring the house?"

"In the neighborhood of seventy-five thousand," Travis said.

Abbey halted on the L-shaped landing. "That's a heck of a neighborhood. Are you sure it would cost that much?"

"That's a conservative estimate," he said.

Seventy-five thousand! Abbey thought, flinching inside. She didn't doubt what Travis said. She only wondered how she could come up with the money.

She hurried up the last three steps, walked down the hall to the bedroom where she'd slept as child. When she tried to open the door, she found it was warped. It wouldn't budge.

Travis nudged her aside, put his shoulder to the door, forcing it open. He stepped aside to allow Abbey to pass.

Abbey walked directly to the window overlooking the front porch. Close up she could see that the shingles were rotted and the board and tar beneath pitted with holes. Every inch of the house would have to be worked. Why hadn't she seen it before?

Travis joined her at the window. She expected him to point out the needed repair of the roof. She decided to beat him to it.

"I know the—" Abbey said as he began, "It's a wonder we—" They paused, looking at each other. He *hadn't* been going to remark about the condition of the roof, she decided. "You first," she offered eagerly.

"All I was going to say was that it was a wonder we didn't break our necks climbing up and down that cottonwood tree," he said.

Abbey's gaze traveled to the branch that hung over the porch, the one they'd used in shimmying from the main trunk to reach the roof. She chuckled. "I wonder why we thought climbing the tree, crawling across the roof and through the window was easier than walking through a door?"

"It wasn't easier," Travis said, smiling. "It was more fun."

"Right," Abbey agreed.

"Sometime I wonder if I've forgotten how to have fun," he pondered.

It must be their age, Abbey decided. Jill was disgruntled with her personal life. Abbey questioned her relationships with men. Now Travis wondered if he'd forgotten how to have fun.

"You have to admit that there's a difference between the kind of fun we had as kids and the kind of fun we have as adults," she observed.

"Isn't that what I said?" Travis asked, his gaze meeting hers. It was too serious, Abbey thought. "Children have spontaneous fun. As adults we make a project of it. We plan when we're going to have fun. Or don't you find that to be true?"

"Yes," Abbey said. "I agree. But if a person is mature, responsible, wouldn't spontaneous fun seem a bit silly?"

Travis groaned dramatically. He laughed. "I thought you of all people would understand. But you're in as much danger as I am, Abbey."

"For heaven's sake, in danger of what?"

"In danger of growing old in your mind," Travis said. He tapped his temple with his finger, then his chest. "And here."

Abbey laughed, but nervously. She did know what he was talking about. That was why she so enjoyed being with Cassie and Bob. They could laugh at themselves, enjoy that spontaneity Travis was talking about.

"Do you remember the night I sneaked over here to get you to go to the cemetery?" Travis asked.

His chest was heaving with contained laughter. He brushed his hair away from his forehead. Abbey recalled how Travis had learned that Bob, Cassie and Jill were planning to sneak out after their folks were asleep to play hide-and-seek in the cemetery. Bob had asked if Travis wanted to go. Travis had told him no.

"I remember it, all right! You scratched on the screen to wake me up, told me to get a sheet because we were going to go play ghost. And I went, even though I knew I'd be in a big bunch of trouble if the folks caught me."

"We scared the pants off them, didn't we?" Travis asked.

Abbey chuckled. They'd risen from behind tombstones, waving their arms. "I'd say so," she said.

Travis laughed. "My God. I've never seen such panic. The way they screamed and scattered. Bob still gets mad when I bring it up."

Abbey's laughter tickled her stomach. It was the greatest trick she and Travis had ever pulled on their friends.

"I thought for sure the screaming was going to wake everyone in town," she said.

Travis shook his head. "If it hadn't been for Kitty Bryant, we'd have gotten away with it," he said.

"Have you ever heard anyone beller, 'Ma,' the way she did?"

He laughed again. Abbey gnawed her lip. "We shouldn't be laughing about Kitty. Poor little kid was only seven."

"Her parents should have known better than to trust Jill to babysit her," Travis said. "When Mrs. Bryant called the house the next morning to talk to Dad, I tried to tell him that...that Kitty wouldn't have been scared to death if Jill hadn't been babysitting her."

Abbey's lips trembled. "He didn't buy it?"

"No way. I caught hell in a big way."

Laughter suddenly seemed the furthest thing from Abbey's mind. Kitty's mother had seen Abbey's father in town. He'd come home and used the switch on her.

"One second you're laughing, the next you look very sad," Travis said softly. "What are you thinking?"

He raised his hand as if to touch her cheek, but instead dropped his hand and moved across the room, toward the east window, leaving Abbey bouncing on a wave of emotions.

No one could sense what she felt as he did, she admitted to herself. The knowledge was definitely discomforting. "I was remembering Dad hadn't used the switch on me in years, but he used it after Mrs. Bryant talked to him," she said.

"I didn't know that," Travis said.

"You never told me you'd gotten into trouble with your dad, either," Abbey stated.

"I was too embarrassed," he admitted easily. "I'd come up with the scheme, convinced you it was workable, and when it backfired, I was too proud to admit I wasn't the *man* I thought I was."

Abbey nodded. "Same here. At twelve how could I admit that I'd been spanked?"

Travis looked out the window, then turned to lean against the wall. "Had Lemont been drinking?" he asked.

"He'd had a few, but he wasn't drunk," Abbey said. She sighed. "You know Dad wasn't mean. The switching didn't hurt, but it stung like crazy."

"I can tell something about what happened hurt you enough so that it still bothers you," Travis stated. "If it wasn't the switching, what was it?"

Abbey rubbed her hands together. "What's bothering me is how Mother reacted. She asked why I would have done such a thing. Naturally, I told her that it had been your idea. She told me not to blame you, that I had a mind of my own, to think for myself or I'd always be in trouble," Abbey said. "Then she told Dad to go ahead and whip me, because someone had to get my attention."

"It isn't easy to handle rejection by someone you love," Travis said softly.

For a long moment they were silent, looking across the expanse of the room. He did look as if he understood rejection. But could he really understand? Abbey wondered. Her mother hadn't rejected her. Her mother had loved her.

The only rejection had come from her father and Travis. Her father's rejection had hurt, but she'd

learned how to handle it once she'd understood her
father didn't have the capacity to love.

With Travis's rejection she'd suffered agonizing
mental pain, worse than any physical pain she'd ever
felt. It had been that kind of torment because she'd
believed Travis's capacity to love was infinite.

"I don't think Mother was rejecting me," she said.
"But I knew that I'd failed to live up to her expectations for me."

Travis's brow furrowed. "I offer a belated apology
for being the reason for your failure to live up to your
mother's expectations," he said.

Abbey didn't miss the sarcasm. She wondered what
she'd said to bring such a sharp reproach from him.
"You're forgiven," she said, forcing lightness into her
voice. "What are you going to ask me for the land?"

His jaw muscles tightened. "You believe in jump-
ing right into it, don't you? So the answer is this. If I
were considering selling it, I'd be talking one hundred
thousand an acre."

Abbey leaned against the wall, feeling weak-kneed.
When she'd left Minneapolis she believed two hundred
thousand would cover the entire project.

"That's what the land is worth to us. You're talking three acres at least. Three hundred thousand."

"Okay," Abbey said. "It's worth one hundred
thousand an acre to you. To me the value is more and
I'll come up with the money somehow."

"What do you make a year? Fifty thousand?"

"Close enough. What's the point?"

"The point is I know you made the final payment
only last year on what your dad owed on your mother's hospital bill."

"Who told you?"

"I've been on the hospital board for six years," Travis said. "When you told the administrator you'd like to arrange to pay the debt in monthly installments, he asked us to approve the request. We did, even though you were under no legal obligation to pay it."

"When Mother realized Dad wasn't going to pay the bill, she asked me to do it someday," Abbey said. "When I could."

"Did she ask you to pay Doc Seth? The Feed Elevator? The rent your dad owed Clara?"

Abbey wasn't sure she liked the tone of his voice. Somewhere in it were accusation, anger. "Mother didn't like taking charity. I don't like taking charity. That's why I paid those debts."

"There's been something I never understood," Travis said. "Why did Jen feel you had to leave Beaver Crossing to make something of yourself?"

Abbey was sure now she didn't like his tone of voice. "Why bring that up?"

"I'm curious."

"It should be obvious to you," Abbey said more tersely than she'd intended. "Dad was an alcoholic. No matter how I tried to please him, no matter how Mother tried, he didn't care about anything but where his next drink was coming from."

Her lips trembled, but she was determined not to choke. "Mother wanted something better for me than she'd had. She knew with the farm gone, there was nothing for me in Beaver Crossing, no way for me to regain the respect Dad had lost. It was either leave

Beaver Crossing or forever be known as *poor little Abbey*."

"And you aren't set on buying the farmstead to prove you aren't poor little Abbey?" he asked.

Abbey planted her feet squarely, folded her arms at her waist. "Do you actually believe my motive is so self-serving and shallow?"

Travis's gaze held Abbey gently. "No," he said. "I have always known you had soul. I have always known you were singularly remarkable. I have always respected you. You had nothing to prove to me."

His gaze was like a glove of tenderness embracing Abbey. She really had not known he thought she was remarkable. She turned, looking out the window.

Did it matter how he felt? In the end, her dependency on him had resulted in her loss of self-respect.

"Those are lovely sentiments," she said. "And I'm moved by them. But they're meaningless, I'm afraid. When it came right down to it, I had something to prove to myself."

Travis moved from where he'd been standing and walked toward the door. He desperately wanted to ask Abbey if she'd ever thought he was remarkable, if he'd ever had her respect. If, just once, she'd believed all she needed to make herself feel whole was for him to love her.

But he wouldn't ask. He knew how he'd felt had been important to her, only not as important to her as pleasing Jen, living up to Jen's expectations.

Whether Abbey accepted it or not, she was still a captive of the past, a captive of what Jen had wanted for her, not what she wanted for herself. But it was futile to talk about it.

"What next?" he asked. "The barn?"

Abbey turned from the window. "Sure," she said.

She knew the inspection of the barn wouldn't take long. While she went inside, Travis lingered in the doorway and refrained from commenting. She was thankful for that.

She climbed the ladder until her head was even with the floor of the loft, then glanced up through the dust to the high rafters. There were several huge holes in the roof.

She dropped to the floor and walked along the row of cow stanchions. Her father had talked about replacing the wooden stanchions with steel. He'd never done it. She stopped at the stanchions where her cows, Daisy and Belinda, had been stalled. She touched the slivered wood, remembering the feel of the heat given off by the cows' bodies on a cold winter morning. She could still feel the coarseness of their hair as she pressed her forehead against their bellies, could still smell their pungent aroma, the sweet smell of wheat straw.

She'd milked the two cows twice a day while her father milked eight. He'd never missed morning milking. Sometimes he was so hung over that he would have to stop for a drink from the bottle he always had hidden somewhere in the barn, but he never missed the morning milking.

He seldom remembered to come home in time for the evening chores. Her mother had milked the eight cows then. When her mother got too sick to do the milking, Abbey milked alone.

She would milk as fast as she could, but before she'd finish, the cows would be bawling from full and painful bags and she'd be crying in frustration.

She moved to where Travis waited. "The barn will have to be razed," she said. "And renovation of the house is going to cost more than I'd planned."

Travis stepped into the sunlight. "The buildings are coming down, Abbey."

"You're not going to discuss it?" Abbey asked.

He turned to face her. "You aren't discussing it. You're telling me what to do."

"You're forcing me to tell you, forcing me to talk to Roy," she said.

"I'm not forcing you."

"Your dad made a promise to my mother."

"He told a dying woman what he knew she wanted to hear," Travis said, sounding genuinely sad.

"Roy thought of my mother as *poor* Jen? He pitied her?" Abbey asked.

"Get off the pity kick," Travis said evenly.

# Chapter Seven

"Well, excuse me for thinking pity was involved," Abbey said menacingly. Forget maturity. Forget position. Forget control. She wanted to pop him anywhere she could land a clean blow. "Weren't you the one who was always saying you felt sorry for me?"

"I felt bad when you felt bad," Travis said. "Like when you had the lead in a class play, or made the honor roll and Lemont was never there to cheer you on. But I did *not* pity you. You had too much pride to allow me to pity you."

"Mother called it Penny pride," Abbey said.

"I remember," Travis said. "A Penny might not have a penny, but a Penny had pride."

"You think I had too much pride, don't you?" Abbey asked.

Travis laughed gruffly. "I'm not stupid enough to answer that question."

"You're right. It was a catch-22," Abbey said. "But now I'm wondering if pride doesn't have something to do with my wanting the buildings."

Travis's face paled, and deep lines were etched around his eyes and lips. "Don't bring it up again, Abbey," he pleaded. "We'll end up saying hurtful things to each other and I can't handle it. Not anymore."

He turned, walked briskly toward his pickup.

Abbey was stunned. She didn't want to hurt him, either. They had hurt each other enough. But she felt an urgency to talk, sort through the debris, reach some sort of understanding.

Even though she couldn't begin to guess what kind of understanding they could reach, she couldn't allow him to go. Not this way.

"Travis! Wait!" He stopped, turned. "Tomorrow morning. Eight o'clock," she said.

"What?"

"At eight o'clock tomorrow morning," she said, "please say we can talk about it again. After we've had time to think it over, get our emotions under control."

"Are we scheduling an argument?" he asked.

She closed the distance between them, stopping short of confronting him. "Maybe you have a better idea."

"A better idea would be to drop it."

"I know the barn can't be restored, but maybe you'd consider a compromise," she said, more grasping at straws than thinking the idea was workable. "Maybe you'd consider selling me the house."

"All I can promise is that I'll think about discussing it," he said, then continued to the pickup, slipped inside and started it.

He was leaving! The least he could have done was said goodbye. She flagged him down. When he leaned out the window, she said, "I didn't say goodbye."

"It sounded like goodbye to me," Travis said.

He wasn't going to help her out, Abbey thought. "What about dinner?"

"Considering what happened the last time we were at Irene's, I thought you'd feel more comfortable if I weren't there tonight," he said.

Relief flooded through Abbey. So that was what he'd been thinking, not that he had *other* plans. "I'll admit when Bob first brought up the subject of eating at Irene's, all I could do was think about the last time we were there. But I can handle it if you can."

"We do have to let go of the past, don't we?" Travis said. A tentative smile came to his lips. "Would I hear one word about buildings?"

"I'm willing to bend, Travis. I'm not willing to break. The agreement is no argument, *providing* we discuss it in the morning," she said firmly, hoping he would also bend.

"You drive a tough bargain," he said. "Okay. I'll see you around nine. That is, unless you find yourself looking for something to do later this afternoon. You could come to the pit. I'd like to show you around."

Excitement beat in Abbey's chest. She felt as if he were asking her out on a date. Belatedly she realized why she'd stopped him, why she'd suggested they meet, compromise. She wanted to be with him—too much.

"You know how Clara likes to visit," she said. "But I'll see."

Travis turned the pickup around. Dust drifted up as he departed, leaving Abbey with her feet planted squarely in the middle of the farmstead.

She looked north to where her father had once planted corn or harvested soybeans. She could see the glistening water, the Matthews pit on Penny land.

She tried to envision the row of cottonwood trees gone. The barn gone. The hog house and chicken house gone. And the windmill. She tried to envision water lapping at her feet.

She knew she could wear Travis down. She could win. But why was she feeling that in winning, she'd lose?

Abbey drove to the Dillers, washed, changed into a yellow gauze blouse and fresh jeans, then brushed her hair. She walked across town to see Clara, taking a route past the school playground.

She stopped to watch a group of young children playing. A little girl pumped a swing, singing, "I'm touching the sky!" Another sat, the swing idle, looking up to the sky. Dreaming? Abbey wondered. Or checking to see whether or not her playmate's pointed toes were touching the clouds?

Two little boys stood close to the swing, watching.

One of the boys smacked an imaginary horse. He galloped away, calling excitedly, "The cattle are stampeding! Let's go!" The second boy, whooping, "I'll get 'em," took off.

Chuckling, Abbey walked on. She was sure she'd heard those conversations before. Only the names had been changed. Travis was right about spontaneous fun. He was right about a lot of things.

She reached Clara's house. Her father, Mr. Markroy, had founded the bank, and the house he'd built for his family was a three-story mansion with a ballroom on the third floor. The front door was oak. The entablature was set off by a hand-carved cornice. There were six Palladian windows, three on each side of the door. The hand-carved design was continued on the window cornices.

"Land, child," Clara said when she opened the door in response to Abbey's knock. "Get your body in here and give me a squeeze."

Abbey stepped into the hall, took Clara's frail body into her arms and hugged her. She grinned. "I hear a lot has happened since I talked to you."

"You've heard Tommy's back," Clara said, feigning shucks. But the excitement in her voice, the smile in her eyes couldn't be hidden. She laced her arm with Abbey's. "Come," she said, leading Abbey down the long hall. "He's in the kitchen. We're having milk and cookies."

"Love," she said as she shoved the swinging door open, "Abbey's come to visit."

Tom Green was sitting with his back to the door. Bald and wrinkle-necked and very thin—those were Abbey's first impressions, but as he shifted on the chair, turning toward the door, those impressions faded. The eyes behind the bifocals were blue, alert and expressive.

It barely registered with Abbey that Tom Green had lost one leg below the knee. She might not have realized it at all, except for his crutches leaning against the table.

"Lowell and Mable Penny's granddaughter," Tom said as he straightened in the chair. "Clara said you were the spitting image of your grandma."

Abbey crossed the room and shook Tom's hand. "So I've been told. It's nice to meet you, Tom."

Clara chuckled. "Abbey's too polite to say that she thought you were dead."

Tom laughed. Clara brushed his cheek with a kiss and walked to the cupboard. "Milk?" she asked Abbey.

Abbey nodded, then settled on a chair opposite Tom. Clara set a glass of milk in front of her.

"Clara tells me you travel around the world, buying clothes for the Hesston stores," Tom said. "Mighty impressive."

"Mighty impressive," Clara agreed, "but what Abbey always talked about doing was having her own store. And that's what she should do." Clara emphasized the statement by pointing a thin finger at Abbey.

"It was the dream of a high school student," Abbey said. "Not that I've given it up, but it's a dream for the future. For someday."

"Can't live without our dreams, can we?" Tom offered.

For the next fifteen minutes, while Abbey ate too many chocolate chip cookies and drank two glasses of milk, Tom and Clara peppered her with questions about her work.

Then Clara asked, "Are you into that new apartment?"

"I'm there," Abbey said, "but I haven't had time yet to purchase the furniture I need."

"I know you need a china cabinet, so plan on taking the china cabinet from the dining room. And the cherrywood bedroom set you used while you were staying with me," Clara said.

"I can't do that!" Abbey protested.

"You don't like them?" Clara asked.

"I love them! But they're antiques, worth a small fortune and you'd have an empty bedroom—"

"There are going to be six empty bedrooms before long, because we're going to sell this house and move into the bungalow your folks rented from me," Clara said.

"It's because of me," Tom said. He patted the thigh of his missing leg. "Even when I'm wearing my artificial leg, getting up and down the steps is hard for me."

"Don't you listen to him," Clara said. "He gets around better than I do. The truth is I've rambled around in this old house too long. Only bad memories haunt the halls."

"Now darlin', don't get started," Tom said softly. "Don't upset yourself."

"The only good memories I have are from when we were together on that farm south of town," she said. "And the memories we're making now."

Mesmerized, Abbey listened as Clara and Tom talked about themselves as they'd been. Clara, headstrong and spoiled, had attended high school at an exclusive girls' school in the East. When she graduated and came back to Beaver Crossing to visit before going on to get a teacher's certificate, she met Tom at a barn dance.

Tom was a farmer, a sharecropper. But Clara fell in love at first sight. In spite of her parents' warning that she'd never be happy as the wife of a farmer, she'd married Tom. Then she'd set out to change him. Everything from the clothes he wore to his occupation.

Tom knew he'd never get rich farming, but he refused to take money from Clara's father or to work for him at the bank. He'd heard there was land in Canada to homestead. He told Clara he was going and wanted her to come with him.

She'd said no. She thought he'd miss her, change his mind and come home. Tom thought he'd make his fortune, come back to Beaver Crossing and take her back with him.

He made his fortune, not in farming, but in lumber. In the process he'd lost his leg in a logging accident. Thinking he was only half a man, he didn't return to Clara. And Clara, too proud to admit her husband had left her, had allowed people to think she was a widow.

"Forty years ago I built a house," Tom said. "Built it big. Built it to last, thinking Clara would join me someday. Not long ago I was sitting in the den, listening to nothing but the quiet, and I got to thinking about Clara. And all at once it came to me that if I held on to my pride much longer I was going to be buried with it, not beside the woman I loved."

Tom laid his gnarled hand over Clara's. The smiles in their eyes said it all. Abbey felt her eyes dampen.

When she left the Greens, she was in a subdued, thoughtful mood. How could two people who loved each other so much have been so filled with pride that neither had yielded until it was almost too late?

"If that's all, I'll be leaving," Meg said.

Travis looked up to where Meg was standing. On Saturdays the office help left at two. "Is Garnet gone?"

"About five minutes ago," Meg said. "Anything I can do?"

"Do you know how to enter inventory on the computer?" Travis asked.

"No better than you do," Meg said. "Are you going to try your luck?" She laughed.

"Guess I'll just put this information on hold until Monday," Travis said, grinning. "Have a good weekend."

Meg disappeared. Travis glanced out the window when she walked past to get into her car. When she drove out, his pickup was the only vehicle left in the parking lot.

Maybe he should give up gracefully, admit that Abbey wasn't coming. Why should she come? He'd already agreed to have dinner with them tonight and to "discuss" the Penny place with her in the morning.

She'd have plenty of time then to try out new angles on him. The telephone rang.

"Matthews Sand and Gravel. Travis speaking."

"Did you have time to look?" Bob asked.

"Look for what?"

"That twenty-five-gallon aquarium Christina used to have. You weren't listening to me, were you?" Bob asked.

"I'm listening. But you aren't making much sense."

Bob laughed. "I'm talking about our conversation at lunch. I told you I'd ordered half a dozen lobsters and needed a holding tank. I asked about the aquarium. You told me you'd check your folks' basement to see if it was there."

Travis knew he'd been preoccupied. But he couldn't have been that spaced-out. "Maybe you told one of the women," he suggested.

"Yeah. Like I'd ask Jill to fly one in from Arizona or ask Abbey to deliver one from Minneapolis," Bob said. "And besides, I know exactly when we talked about it. The women had gone back outside after they'd helped carry dishes in. You stayed to talk while I loaded the dishwasher."

"Good grief, yes," Travis said. "I do remember."

"Bingo!" Bob said. "But don't feel bad. Abbey was playing mental solitaire, too."

"I'll admit I was preoccupied. The problem with the auger. I was wondering if the men had it going," Travis said. "When do you need the aquarium?"

"Like today. The lobsters weren't supposed to be delivered until Monday morning, but the truck just dropped them off," Bob said. "Right now they're crawling around the storage room and spooking the help."

Travis snickered.

"You see something funny about lobsters on the loose?"

"Nope. I'll check right away."

"No hurry," Bob said. "Later today is fine. Just let me know if you can't find it. I'll have to arrange to do something else with them."

"Okay."

"Got that?"

"Got it," Travis said.

"Maybe you should tie a string around your finger," Bob said.

"I'll remember."

"You might get preoccupied. Abbey's still around and you might get tense about the auger again—"

"Cut the sarcasm," Travis said. "I was thinking about Abbey. She's determined to get in the way of my razing the buildings. Have you ever had the awful feeling you were headed for disaster but couldn't stop yourself?"

"Sure."

"You did? When?"

"When Cassie told me to marry her or get out of her life," Bob said.

"For crying out loud, Bob!" Travis snapped. "I'm talking about the Penny place. The only reason Abbey's being decent to me is because she thinks she can get me to change my mind."

"From the way Abbey's gaze kept drifting to you, I'd say you're on her mind, and for reasons that don't have to do with the farmstead."

Travis leaned back in the chair, spinning a ballpoint pen between his thumb and index finger. "You're on the wrong track, Bob. It didn't work for Abbey and me ten years ago. And it wouldn't work out now," Travis said.

"She hurt you more than you want to admit, didn't she?"

"Let's just say that she hurt me bad enough that I'm not going to let her do it again."

## Chapter Eight

He wasn't going to let Abbey hurt him again, Travis thought. But after Bob's call he didn't leave the office. Instead he hung around, pacing in front of the window, looking up the lane with each car passing, wondering if she was coming.

He was beginning to think Abbey was right. Maybe their having been with each other constantly had been a habit. A bad habit. Like smoking. He'd started in college. Three years ago he'd decided to break the habit. After days and months of nerve-jangling denial he'd believed he was free of the craving.

Then he'd accepted an after-dinner smoke from a business associate. And the craving was back, raging worse than before. He'd quit again last year.

But that was how it was with Abbey. There'd been no satisfaction in seeing her once or twice. He wanted more.

He could use a cigarette now.

Too late. Abbey's car had pulled into view.

Travis pushed the door open before she reached the building and held it open. "I'm glad you came," he said.

"What happened to all the people?" she asked.

"We close at two on Saturdays."

Abbey walked into the building, turned toward Travis when he let the door whoosh closed. "But you're still working?"

"Still working," he said.

"If you're busy—"

"It can wait. Let me give you the ten-cent tour. How much have you seen of the office?"

"Your office, the reception area," Abbey said, wondering what had happened now. Why he seemed so stiff and formal.

He took her arm to guide her down the hall. He showed her the conference room. The lighting fixtures were recessed, a huge, mountain mural covered one wall. The furnishings were oak. Farther on there was a lunchroom, complete with hidden sink, refrigerator and microwave.

"This is the main office," Travis said, opening another door. There were six computer stations. "Each of the pits has its own supervisor. But we handle purchasing, sales, scheduling rail hopper car dispersions and truck deliveries through here. Until we set this system up, I didn't realize how many man-hours we were wasting."

"Any men working in the office?" Abbey asked, smiling.

"And *women*-hours we were wasting," Travis said. "Three men work in the office. And there are five women drivers."

"Because you're an equal opportunity employer?" Abbey asked.

"Because the women are excellent drivers," Travis said. "They have a gentle hand, don't rip the guts out of their trucks. And when a truck is on the road hauling, it's making money. When it's sitting in the shop, it's not."

"I stand corrected and informed," Abbey said easily. "You really enjoy this, don't you? You're content."

She was referring to his work, Travis knew. But he was looking into her eyes and struggling with himself. He wanted to tell her that he'd realized how discontented he was with his personal life.

"I'm happy helping Dad run the business," he said.

"There was a time when you didn't know what you wanted out of life."

He laughed, leaned against the doorjamb. "I always knew what I *wanted* out of life."

Abbey read innuendo in his eyes. Her heart pounded, and her mind beamed a singular thought— she was what he had always wanted.

That was probably true, she conceded. At least physically it was true. She moved to a desk, checked the computer out.

"So you always knew what you wanted out of life," she said. "I certainly wouldn't question your veracity, but there were times when you sounded like a modern Shakespeare. To get a degree in business or not to get a degree in business, that is the question."

Travis laughed. "Yes, Abbey. That was the question I banged around aloud. But the one I should have been asking was the one I was thinking—Why go to college at all, when what I really want to do is work with Dad?"

He led her back down the hall.

"Why didn't you say so?" Abbey asked as they stepped from the office into the sunlight.

"Because you made me feel as if staying here wasn't the noblest of objectives."

"I don't remember ever saying anything like that. I wouldn't have said it," she stated decisively.

"Maybe it was your attitude," Travis conceded. "You had all those plans about going to college, finding your niche in the world of fashion, and all I wanted to do was work with Dad. It made me feel as if I was planning on amounting to nothing."

Abbey laughed before she saw he was serious. "I never knew," she said. "I didn't. I thought you wanted to go to college."

"College was more the folks' idea than mine," Travis said dryly. "They kept telling me an education wouldn't kill me. And they were right. It didn't kill me. In fact, after a certain time of adjustment I enjoyed it."

Abbey wondered whether she'd enjoyed college or simply put in time because it was something she had to do in order to get where she was going. She hadn't enjoyed the first year. She'd been so mired in missing Travis and in being miserable, she hadn't enjoyed anything.

As they walked, wherever Abbey looked there were draglines, hydraulic shovels, gravel trucks. On the railroad spur there were more hopper cars than she had time to count, each carrying the Matthews name.

"I'd heard you'd put Matthews Sand and Gravel on the map," she said, gesturing to the rail spur. "Rolling advertisement of the fact. And I'm only seeing a small part of the operation, aren't I?"

"You're seeing the biggest part of it. Our main business is supplying gravel and rock for road construction. We use this pit exclusively for that," Travis said. "The other pits supply sand and gravel needed for smaller projects, the kind of things Dad built the business on. Everything from gravel used in distribution fields for septic tank beds to footing for foundations and concrete bricks."

"I noticed that the pit on the Penny place isn't being worked," she said as she followed him toward a large corrugated metal building. "Why?"

"We worked the veins that were viable. They ran out three years ago," Travis explained. "On the south eighty acres of the Penny place our surveys indicate only isolated acres of deposits. Not worth the investment it would take to work it. We rent the farmland out."

"But the land where the buildings sit," Abbey stated, "has gravel under it."

"Rock," Travis said. "The kind that makes an excellent road base when crushed."

"So that's why you've decided you have to clear the farmstead. To get to the veins of rock."

"I thought we were saving the arguments until tomorrow morning," Travis said.

"It was a question," Abbey said. "For my enlightenment."

"The state asked for bids on completing the inter-state highway into Minnesota. I got the contract to supply the crushed rock. And the kind of rock I need is under the farmstead."

"What about the pits north of town on the Han-cock and Reynold places?" she asked. "Couldn't you get rock from them?"

"The deposits north of town are basically sand and coarse gravel," he said. He stopped before the door, turned and gestured to the bluffs. "The loess hills end where the county road heads out of Beaver Crossing. The rock deposits in this area start here and run south. The only rock I own is on this place or the Penny place. And this pit is running low."

Abbey's heart plummeted as Travis spoke.

"My back is against the wall, Abbey. Maybe I was wrong to make the bid to the state without consulting you, but I honestly believed you didn't want the Penny place."

He grabbed the handle of one of the double doors. Inside sat a twin-engined plane.

"Want to go get a bird's-eye view of the valley?" he asked.

"I'd rather not," she said.

"Are you saying that because you're angry with me?" he asked.

"Why would I be angry?"

"Because I told you I had to have the rock—"

"Oh, no," Abbey rushed to assure him. "I believe you when you say you didn't think I wanted the buildings. I said no to flying because I really don't en-joy it."

"You've flown to Europe, California. . . ."

"Sure I have." Abbey laughed. "I fly often, but I never look forward to it. Every time the plane taxies for takeoff, I feel a terrible surety it isn't going to get enough steam to lift off. With every landing I feel a terrible surety we're going to end up in the terminal."

"But you'll go with me," Travis stated.

He won her with his smile, his confidence in her to respond to his need to have her with him. "Okay," she said.

"You don't sound enthusiastic."

"After the coercion, I didn't know you wanted enthusiasm," she said.

"If you believe it was coercion, maybe enthusiasm was too much to ask for," he said. "Maybe a compromise? How about a little smile?"

She placed her index fingers at the corners of her mouth and pulled her lips into a smile. "Thee. Thmiling face."

Travis laughed. "Okay. Let's do it."

As he taxied the plane to the private runway behind the hangar, the sound of its engines was low, steady. Abbey waited for the familiar foreboding to come over her. It didn't.

But she'd known she wouldn't feel it. As when she'd followed him into the basement, she trusted his lead. She trusted him to get the plane up. She trusted him to get the plane down. She drew the line there. She'd never trust him with her heart again.

He revved the engines, reached for the control levers, and the ground began moving beneath them. When she felt her stomach shifting, she closed her eyes.

"You can open your eyes now," Travis said.

"Where are we?"

"Cruising northwest of Beaver Crossing. Out about fifteen miles," Travis said.

"I know you're laughing at me," Abbey said.

"You'll never know for sure if you don't open your eyes and look."

Smiling, she opened her eyes. "I knew you were laughing. So I feel obligated to remind you that I remember a time when you weren't so cotton-picking brave."

"I was always brave."

"Scoffing laugh." Abbey laughed. "We were riding the roller coaster in the amusement park outside Des Moines."

"I had my eyes open," Travis said.

"What does that prove? You turned a sickly blue," Abbey said. "And it has just occurred to me that I must be crazy. Why would I trust my body to a man who can't ride a roller coaster?"

"You're right," Travis said, grinning. "Why would you?"

He circled back toward Beaver Crossing. Abbey worked her jaws, popped her ears as he dropped the plane over the South Dakota bluffs and into the Big Sioux Valley.

She leaned closer to the passenger window and peered down. They were flying low. Hovering, it seemed. Tractors were pulling planters. Since it was April, it had to be corn being planted. The plane wings wavered. She turned to Travis.

"Did you do that on purpose? Or did we hit an air pocket?"

"Al Meeker waved to us," Travis said. His teeth were exposed in a a broad grin. "You remember Al, don't you?"

"If that was Al on the tractor, he didn't wave."

"I didn't turn a sickly blue," Travis challenged.

Abbey knew, she just knew he was going to waggle the wings again if she maintained that he had. "Actually," she said slowly, "you were purple. A ghastly purple."

The wings wavered again. "Sam Jones," Travis said.

Abbey was threatened by a fit of giggling. "Sam Jones, my foot," she sputtered. "You were purple, but you looked good in purple."

"I think I see Ralph—"

"You're risking our lives," Abbey warned.

"You know better than that," Travis said, his tone low, impassioned. "I'd never jeopardize your safety."

Abbey nodded, looked out her window. He never would. Even when he'd felt obligated to her, he'd been trying to protect her. "Do you think there's any possibility that after tomorrow we can walk away as friends?" she asked.

Travis pushed the throttle forward, sent the plane arching upward, then banked. Walk away this time as friends? he wondered. On the surface the statement sounded naive. Friends. After what they'd been to each other.

"You didn't answer," Abbey said.

He took a deep breath. "I didn't because I thought you wouldn't like hearing what I had to say."

Abbey wasn't dumb. He'd answered. When he'd kissed her, she'd known exactly what about her still interested him—and it wasn't friendship. But she'd made the overture. She'd offered the possibility of forgiving each other.

"We're over the Hancock and Reynold places," he said.

Abbey leaned to look out her window. The pit lakes were small in comparison to the Matthews pit she could see looming ahead. And the pit on the Penny place looked like a water puddle.

"How many acres do the pits cover?" she asked.

"The pits north of town about fifty. Matthews Lake is close to a hundred. Penny Lake about fifteen," he said.

"Penny Lake?" Abbey asked.

"Penny Lake is the name I gave for the plat map," he said.

Soaring birds couldn't have outraced the rapid ascent of Abbey's spirits. Penny Lake. Penny Lake! "I love it," she said.

By the time they'd landed and secured the plane, the sun was going down. Their conversation had drifted easily from one topic to another. They argued once, briefly and heatedly, but by the time Abbey climbed from the plane, she couldn't remember why.

She said a reluctant goodbye and left for the Dillers to clean up for dinner. It had been a tiring day physically, yet she was looking forward to dinner, to being with Travis. So much was familiar about him. So much was new and challenging.

When she arrived at the Dillers, the house was empty. She didn't mind. She needed the quiet. Time to unwind. She drew a full tub of water, loaded it with bubble bath and climbed in, sinking to her chin.

The telephone rang just as she was slipping into a fresh pair of jeans and a peach-colored blouse. She picked up the phone in the hall. "Diller residence. Abbey speaking."

"Hello, Abbey."

"Hello, Travis," Abbey said, smiling.

"You're smiling, aren't you?"

"What makes you think so?"

"I hear it."

"You're right," Abbey agreed.

"So you're happy that I called?"

"I'm happy anyone called," she teased. "Bob isn't home from the store yet. Jill hasn't shown up, and this house seems so big and so darn quiet."

"All alone and lonesome?"

"All alone and lonesome," Abbey said lightly, even as a chill ran up her spine. In the Markroy mansion bad memories haunted Clara because she'd been alone.

"I've been thinking," Travis was saying. "About a change in plans for tonight. Instead of going to Irene's, how about dinner at my place?"

Alone with Travis in his bachelor pad? The idea was tempting. "Ah . . . what about the others?"

"I meant them, too. Of course," Travis said. "I'm calling from the store. Bob says he'll tell Jill about the change of plans. I'll swing by the house and pick you up."

"I could drive down."

"It would be a waste of gas. You can ride down with me and come back with the others. I'll pick you up in ten minutes."

*  *  *

"I can't believe your house is down here," Abbey said. "Anywhere."

Travis chuckled. The lane had dropped from the bluff road, plunging into sweeping curves into an ocean of trees. "Believe me," he said, "it's just around this next corner."

So far he hadn't made a foolish statement, hadn't touched her. The moment she'd left the pit, he'd wondered why he hadn't. And while he had been thinking that, he'd admitted to himself that two hours until he saw her again was too long to wait.

So he'd rushed to his parents' house, found the aquarium, taken a quick shower and changed into clean jeans and shirt from the clothes he kept there. He'd taken the aquarium to Bob and concocted the idea of dinner at his house...because he wanted to touch Abbey and because he wanted her to see where he lived.

The earth home built into the side of the bluff appeared. The facade was a combination of redwood log and colonnades of rock and glass exposed to the south. He parked, waited for her to say whether or not she approved.

"It's absolutely beautiful," Abbey said. She eased from the pickup, closed the door. "Whenever I'm in Beaver Crossing, I reflect how quiet it is, but the quiet here is majestic."

She looked at him, smiling, then away. He knew she was taking in details, everything from the native grass, flowers and trees he'd maintained, to the way the setting sun was casting long shadows.

And Travis took in details about Abbey—from the way her fingers waved in the air in silent accent to her thoughts to the tilt of her head, when her gaze lingered on something that captured her imagination.

Again Travis wanted to touch her. Because her smile told him she appreciated what he'd created. Or was it because after tomorrow morning he might never get close enough to touch her again?

"Do you miss the rumble of traffic when you're in Beaver Crossing?" he asked casually.

"Never," she said. "It's bad enough in Minneapolis, but when I'm in New York or Paris, the traffic paralyzes me."

Travis smiled at himself. He might forget that she was a world traveler and he was a "stay-at-home," but she wasn't going to allow him to forget it.

Even if he were foolish enough to allow himself to fall in love with her again, that was what they still were—Abbey, saying "I could never be satisfied in Beaver Crossing" and himself, "I could never be satisfied anywhere else."

He walked to the front door and unlocked it, then slipped his keys into his jean-pocket. "You would never allow some little thing like traffic to immobilize you," he said as he pushed the door open.

"Of course not," Abbey said. "I hire a cab and yell over the noise."

"A tightwad like you hires a cab?" Travis asked. He switched on the entry light, stepped inside, held the door open for Abbey.

"The company pays for it. Travis!" She dropped to her knees and ran her fingers over the stone slabs of the entry hall. "This is *real* stone slab!"

"You expected fake?"

She bounced up. "I don't know what I expected . . . but hurry up and switch on the lights so I can see the rest of the house."

Travis stepped to the main panel, turning on one light after another until the house was bathed in a soft glow.

She moved quickly into the great room, looked up at the redwood beams, walked to the stone fireplace and touched the rock. "This looks like the rocks from—"

"It *is* from the Penny place," he said.

She glanced over her shoulder, her expression unreadable. "You'll light a fire later, won't you?" she asked.

"Sure," Travis said.

The next thing he knew, Abbey had settled in one of the oversize chairs in the conversation area, wiggled her shoulders, slipped off her loafers and drawn her legs under her. "Heavenly," she said.

"Heavenly?" Travis inquired with a chuckle.

"Most sofas and chairs are too small to be comfortable. But this chair is just right!"

It warmed Travis's heart to see how absolutely right Abbey looked in this house. Right to the core it warmed him.

"Are you playing Goldilocks?"

"I'll play Goldilocks if you'll play the baby bear," she said. She laughed.

Her laughter invited Travis to move closer. He walked to the chair, hovered over her. The warmth he was feeling had turned to a terrible aching. He placed a hand on each arm of the chair, leaned forward.

"Let me choose my own role, Abbey," he said, need driving his voice low.

"You don't want to be a bear?"

Her smile was faint, her voice tremulous. And he damn well should kiss her, he thought. She'd come to his house, knowing they'd play by his rules.

"Right, Abbey," he whispered. "I've outgrown the part of baby bear. I'm better suited now for the role of the wolf."

# Chapter Nine

Travis knew Abbey could be kissed. And he knew she'd kiss him back. And he could make love to her, because making love had never been a problem for them.

The problem came afterward.

And ten years ago he'd been wrong to try to hold her through mutual physical attraction. He'd be as wrong now. That thought was enough to cool his ardor.

He smiled, making it deliberately leering. "This wolf is hungry. How about a quick tour of the house before I fix the pizza I promised Bob?"

Dazed and bewildered, Abbey stumbled after Travis, her bare feet sinking into the thick, spongy carpet. She ran back to retrieve her loafers, then hurried after him.

He hadn't been teasing. He'd wanted to kiss her. He'd been going to kiss her. Only he'd changed his mind. Why? she wondered. Had she scared him away by looking too eager?

Because she was eager. She would have kissed him back, and then some. She caught up with him in the large, fully equipped home office.

The passion he'd felt was now fully in check. He was the gracious, gregarious host as they toured the library, a recreation room complete with billiard table. There were three bedrooms, each with bath.

The dining area and kitchen were one room, separated by a breakfast bar and overhanging cupboard. The room was tied together with redwood beams. The appliances were beige, the gadgetry lemon and the breakfast bar stools a cool green.

"Who did your decorating?" she asked.

"I did," Travis said. "You like the house, don't you?"

Abbey looked to where he was taking food from the refrigerator and setting it on the counter. "You could have settled on building a house," she said. "But you didn't. You made a home."

"I had a woman in mind when I built the house," Travis said. "But it didn't work out."

Which woman had it been? Abbey wondered. She pretended to be studying the stained glass light suspended over the honey oak harvest table in the dining area. Mary Ann? Evelyn?

She turned toward him. "I'm sorry that it didn't work out," she said.

"The odds were against us from the beginning," he said. "She didn't want what I wanted out of life."

His sadness moved Abbey. She couldn't begrudge him happiness. Everyone needed someone. She needed someone. "It happens," she said. "A man and a woman might have a lot in common, but still be heading in different directions in their lives."

Travis nodded. "She never lied to me about what she wanted out of life. But when she left me, I lost my best friend."

"Me," Abbey murmured. "You're talking about me?"

"I didn't know it was you when I was building this," Travis said, sounding her bewilderment. "I honestly didn't. But every beam, every log, every rock, the furnishings, without consciously thinking your name, it was you that I had in mind. I just hadn't realized until I saw how you reacted to the house."

Travis closed the refrigerator and moved to the counter. He'd stumped her, stumped himself. He'd caused tension when the last thing he wanted was tension.

"It isn't unusual that what I chose would be a reflection of you," he said easily. "We liked the same art, the same music, the same books."

"I suppose that's true."

"It's true, Abbey, so rest easy. You can like my house without feeling obligated to like me," he said. "Care to help out by making a fruit salad? You'll find the fixings in the refrigerator."

Abbey didn't ask what kind of fruit salad. She busied herself, opened the refrigerator and set out apples, oranges. "Pears?" she asked.

"Canned. In the pantry," he said.

Abbey washed fruit, sliced and peeled. Drained fruit, sliced and diced. She folded prepared, whipped cream into the mixture.

Travis mixed two grainy pizza doughs, topped one with shrimp, Parmesan and spices; the second he topped with sauerkraut, cheddar and apple.

Abbey placed the finished salad in the refrigerator and cleaned up after herself.

"Would you hand me a beer?" Travis asked.

"I didn't see any in the refrigerator," she said. "Where do you keep it?"

"You'll find what you need behind the doors next to the china cabinet," Travis said. "I have a small refrigerator there."

Abbey went to the cupboard and swung the double doors back. They were lined with glass racks. The selection was as complete as any she'd seen. Snifters, champagne flutes, cocktail glasses. She chose a mug for Travis's beer, then glanced at the filled liquor rack before bending to open the door of the refrigerator.

She took out a can of beer, shut the refrigerator door, then the double doors of the bar unit. He hadn't had her in mind when he'd installed the unit, she thought. He knew how she felt about having alcohol in the house.

She poured the beer, dropped the can into the compactor, then carried the mug to where he was placing the last of the apple slices on the pizza and set the glass where he could reach it.

"Thank you," he said, glancing up. "What's your problem?"

"Problem? I don't have a problem." She climbed onto one of the stools.

"You do have a problem because you're frowning." He set the pizzas aside, took dishcloth from the sink and wiped the counter. "Spit it out."

"I do not have a problem," she said.

Travis rinsed the dishcloth, then his hands, drying them on a paper towel. He picked up the beer mug on his way to the breakfast bar.

"You must entertain *a lot*," she said.

"I entertain frequently. Mostly for business reasons. Is that what's bothering you?" he asked. "That I entertain?"

He settled on the stool next to her, his knee accidentally brushing Abbey's. She moved her knee away. "No, that isn't what was bothering me. I'm just surprised that you asked me to get you a beer."

"You could have told me to get it myself," he said.

"That's not what I mean, either," Abbey said. "I didn't know you drank."

"I have a beer occasionally," he said. "A highball occasionally, but alcohol doesn't govern my life."

Abbey smiled guiltily. "I was on the verge of preaching, wasn't I? Trying to tell you how to live your life."

Travis grinned. "Oh, no. Not you! You'd never try to tell me how to run my life."

"Yes. Me. I have done that from time to time," Abbey said. There was a bubble of warmth building around them. "I was going to tell you that the bar didn't belong in this house."

He teased her with a quick tilt of his head, a sparkle deep in his eyes. "If you were sharing this house with me, I'd ask you for your opinion."

"Would you listen?"

"The bar would vanish," he said, snapping his fingers, "just like that, *if* you were here."

Abbey felt herself slipping toward him. It would be so easy to respond to what she saw in his eyes. "Bob, Cassie and Jill are coming at nine, aren't they?" she asked.

"You know what I'm thinking, don't you?"

She was frantic. "They're late."

"Don't try to change the subject. I would very much like to make love to you."

"Think it. Don't say it."

"I'll think it, I'll say it, but I won't attempt it," Travis said, his voice heavy. "I wouldn't take the chance that you'd hate me tonight. And I know I'd hate myself in the morning."

He'd said those words to her before! The night of their senior prom. He'd struggled to control the need he felt for her. He'd told her that she'd hate him. She'd assured him she wouldn't. She'd kissed him, begged him to hold her.

She took a deep breath, met his gaze, spoke brazenly. "We were virgins, you said. But I always doubted that I was the first."

"How could you say that?"

"From the first real kiss you gave me, you knew what you were doing. I didn't," she stated.

"When we were sophomores? After the football game?"

"Yes. You were so confident."

"I wasn't confident. I was scared. We were best friends," Travis countered. "I didn't think you'd take me seriously. And I was serious. I wanted to be your lover." In the middle of his thought, he suddenly chuckled. "But I did practice kissing you."

"Practiced? On whom?" Abbey asked.

"Not on a whom." He laughed again. He took a long swig of beer. "In front of the mirror. Hours of puckering, trying to see what I was doing through squinted eyes. Which was nearly impossible. That's how experienced I was."

"For heaven's sake," Abbey said. "I wish I'd known that. Maybe I could have slept that night if I had. As it was, I lay awake, thinking how fantastic the kiss had been, but sure you'd never kiss me again because I'd been so stupid."

"You thought it was fantastic?"

"Fantastic."

"You told me it was okay," Travis said. He grinned. "My ego barely survived the trauma of being mediocre."

Though he'd been teasing when he'd said his ego barely survived, Travis was telling the truth. The first kiss—that was when he'd begun feeling ordinary in her eyes. She'd made him feel ordinary when he desperately wanted her to adore him.

She laughed gently, her gaze coddling. "You survived."

"Sure. But why didn't you say how you felt?"

"Alice and Kim were hanging on your shirttails at school," Abbey said. He grinned. "Don't laugh or I won't tell you," she warned.

"I'm only grinning because I didn't think you'd noticed."

"I noticed. Those girls were *juniors*," Abbey said. She was somewhere between laughter and tears, not sure herself in which direction she was moving. "They were *after* you. And they'd had experience with boyfriends."

"That's it?" Travis asked. "End of explanation?"

"Of course not," Abbey said. "Because of them and their experience I *had* to pretend to be blasé. Understand?"

Travis laughed. "You were jealous?"

"I wasn't jealous. I was scared."

"Of me?"

"No. Not of you," Abbey said. "I was afraid that because of my inexperience I'd lose you, my dearest friend, to Alice or Kim."

"They were no threat to you, Abbey," Travis said, his gaze probing every nook and cranny of her mind. "No woman has ever been a threat to your place in my heart. You own it."

She had a place in his heart. And now if he whispered, "Come with me, make love with me," she knew she'd follow him. If he stood, said nothing but offered his hand, she would go with him, because his gaze told her that in some way he still loved her.

"Abbey," he whispered hoarsely. "Don't look at me like that. Just don't do it."

"People, let's eat!" Bob yelled from the front door.

Travis slipped his hand over Abbey's. He squeezed it gently, then went to greet their friends.

Abbey put the pizzas into the preheated oven. Reason told her that in spite of the tenderness, the caring they'd felt, they had been saved from making a mistake both of them would regret in the morning. But she didn't feel relief, only a lack of fulfillment.

When the food was ready, they ate. Played charades. Talked. Laughed. Around one Bob wondered if they shouldn't call it a day. Cassie, yawning, agreed.

"Me, too," Jill said. "Getting up for that 5:00 a.m. flight back to Arizona is going to kill me." She said goodbye to Travis, stood on tiptoe to kiss his cheek, then followed Cassie and Bob out the door.

Abbey and Travis were several steps behind the others. "Thank you for the evening, Travis," she said. "I can't remember when I've had so much fun."

Travis nodded. She was being polite. How much fun could pizza and charades be, compared to a restaurant in New York and a Broadway play?

She stepped ahead of him out the door.

"Want me to pick you up in the morning?" he asked.

"Morning? Oh. Our discussion."

Fight, Travis thought. "We can't talk with Bob and Cassie around. I thought we could go to my office."

"The office will be fine. Good night."

"Good night," Travis said.

He watched until the car lights disappeared, then closed the door. He glanced at his watch. In less than seven hours they would get down to the reason she'd come back to Beaver Crossing.

The second hand swept around, counting down. Eight o'clock and it would be over. He'd never see her again. There was no compromise he could offer.

Abbey didn't toss and turn after going to bed. Moonlight streamed through the window. She lay staring at the ceiling, watching the dancing shadows.

Her mind was focused on Travis. He was shuffling her emotions. She was beginning to lose contact with who she was. She'd worked too hard, driven herself too hard to get where she was to be thinking that she wasn't as happy as she could be, as content as she could be.

She turned her head toward the raised window, thinking she'd heard a sound. She listened, deciding it was the wind rustling leaves.

She willed the speeding thoughts in her mind to slow. She forced her eyes closed. At some point she must have drifted to sleep, because she dreamed Travis was standing on the porch roof, scratching on the screen, whispering, "Abbey? Abbey? Are you sleeping?"

She tossed and turned.

"Abbey. Wake up!"

She opened one eye. The second flew open. She jerked upright, spinning on the bed toward the window. "How did you get there?"

"I climbed a pillar."

"What for?" she whispered.

"I came to get you to play."

She grabbed the sheet, pulling it up to cover her. "You've been drinking!"

He chuckled. "Only the beer I had before dinner," he said.

"Shush! You're talking too loud. You'll wake Cassie and Bob."

"We're wasting time. Get dressed. Meet me at the front door."

"I'm not playing with you."

"Not that kind of playing, Abbey. I mean kid kind of play. Spontaneous—"

"You aren't serious!"

"Abbey," he said slowly, "have you ever wondered if what you're doing is all there is to life?"

He knew which buttons to push. "Can you get off the roof without breaking your neck?" she asked.

"Is that a yes?"

"That's a yes."

Ten minutes later she slipped a ribbon into her jeans pocket, thinking that she might want to tie her hair back later. She crept downstairs and went out the door. She turned and bumped into Travis.

When she gasped, he chuckled. She jabbed his arm. "Funny," she said.

"Come. My car's parked by the garage."

He was walking close, almost but not quite touching her. He guided her to a white convertible.

"Wow," she said. "And I do mean wow."

"You like it?"

"Of course I like it," Abbey said. She opened the door and got in, pulling the door closed behind her.

She waited for Travis to walk around and looked, to find him standing hands on hips. "I *was* going to be a gentleman," he said. "I *was* going to open the door for you. But you didn't trust me to be a gentleman. You just jumped in."

"I'll jump back out," Abbey said and did. She closed the door. "There you go, Travis."

Travis made a chivalrous display of opening the door. "There you go, Abbey."

Abbey slipped back into the car, smiling up at him. "I'm impressed with your urbane manners," she said politely.

"Thank you," he said. He closed the door.

They were still chuckling when Travis turned the key in the ignition and the powerful motor purred. He headed the car south through town.

Travis glanced at Abbey. She was holding her hair back from her face, her expression exhilarated. "What do you do for relaxation?" he asked. "Besides taking trips to New York and Paris?"

Two months ago Abbey had vacationed on Maui. Evan had asked if she would mind if he joined her. She hadn't objected. He'd been a considerate, sweet and entertaining companion—when he'd been with her. Quite often he hadn't been.

They'd taken the hotel van to the dormant volcano Haleakala. He'd chosen to take the van back down the mountain. She'd chosen to make the descent on a bicycle the hotel had provided. He'd stayed at the hotel when she'd gone on a nature hike; he'd chosen to swim in the hotel pool when she'd chosen to locate a pool on 'Ohe'o Stream.

"Trips to Paris and New York aren't pleasure trips but business," she said. "However I vacationed on Maui a couple of months ago."

"Really?" he asked. "I spent a week there a couple of years ago. Did you get a chance to hike up the 'Ohe'o Stream? Swim in one of the pools?"

"As a matter of fact, yes," Abbey said. Had he been alone? She didn't ask. She didn't want to know.

"Did you take the horseback ride through Haleakala?"

"That's one experience I missed," she said.

He described the ride. She closed her eyes to envision it. Envision him. Envision them together on Maui.

"Don't go to sleep on me," he said.

"I won't," she said. "Where are we going?"

"I've had this urge," he said. Abbey held her breath. "To try my hand at skipping pebbles."

Was he trying to entrap her? Abbey wondered. She didn't care. They would have been very good together on Maui. If it had been Travis, not Evan, who'd turned to her as they walked in the moonlight on a sandy beach, she wouldn't have kissed him and wondered why she didn't feel more, wonder if *this* was all there was to life.

She sighed. She'd rejected Evan when he'd tried to make love to her. And if she worked to fall in love with him for a hundred years, it just would not happen.

It wasn't Evan's fault. It was hers. She knew life was a trade-off, a compromise, but she kept wanting everything.

"Skipping pebbles sounds good," she said.

# Chapter Ten

Travis parked in the lane at the Penny place. Walking was no problem. The brilliance of the moon lighted the path. They set off to the creek at a brisk pace.

The breeze caught Abbey's hair, whipping it across her eyes. She brushed it away in an impatient gesture. Then, when she knew it was going to be a nuisance, she dipped into her jeans pocket and came out with the ribbon. She stopped, intending to tie her hair back.

Travis stalled her hand with his, taking the ribbon from her. He laid it around her neck, placed his fingers on either side of her head, spread them and slowly worked her hair back.

"Why would a woman who spent her life trying to set fashion trends stuff a ribbon in her jeans pocket so that it came out wrinkled?" he asked.

Abbey closed her eyes. The massaging of his fingers weakened her knees. She felt wobbly, unstable.

"Split personality," she said lazily. "Does it matter?"

He didn't laugh. He dropped her hair. "Can't do it that way," he murmured. "Turn around."

She did. He slipped up the ribbon and tied it. "Too tight?" he asked.

He wanted to kiss her. She knew it, just as she'd known earlier in the evening. Was he still thinking he'd hate himself in the morning? If it was a problem with him, why had he climbed a porch pillar, scratched on the screen?

Why had he lured her into the night where the moon had painted the sky the color of romance, where the aroma of the air pulsated with it? Why? If he hadn't wanted to make love to her, why was she here?

"The ribbon isn't too tight," she said.

"I didn't do a good job making the bow," he said. "But it's done."

Abbey turned to face him. He'd disciplined his thoughts. His moment of need had passed; hers lingered. But he'd said it was done.

Maybe if she touched him, ran her fingers over his chest, caressed his face.

Her heart urged her to reach for him, but she checked the bow he'd made instead. "Feels good enough to me," she said, dropping her hands.

He tucked a strand of hair he'd missed behind her ear. "You are still a tomboy."

Abbey felt as if his fingers lingered on her cheek stroking, and were stroking through her hair. "In spite of the wrinkled ribbon," she said. "I gave up my tomboy ways about the time I gave up pacing."

He laughed. "You didn't give up pacing. Race you to the mouth of the creek," he challenged.

Abbey thought, Don't panic. Check this out. There had to be a reasonable explanation for her feeling passion one moment and adolescent uncertainty the next.

Was it because she wanted to please him, but he kept changing course? She managed an easy smile, easy words. "Skipping pebbles is one thing," she said. "But race you? No way."

When he was off guard, she sprinted, emitting an unbidden, childish squeal of glee when she felt him closing in on her, protesting she'd cheated.

They reached the mouth of the creek at the same time, collapsed on the bromegrass, laughing. Moments later they'd discarded their shoes, rolled up their jeans and were standing in the creek, water lapping at the calves of their legs.

Abbey bent, slipped her hand through the silky water to the creek bed. More by feel than sight, she located several pebbles. When she straightened, Travis was already bouncing a pebble up and down in the palm of his hand, his expression determined.

"You're sure that I've lost my touch, aren't you?" she asked.

He smiled. "I'm worried that I've lost mine."

Moonlight splashed on the water and was reflected in his eyes. Warm vibrations rippled through Abbey's body. He hadn't lost his touch.

"You first," she said.

He sidearmed the pebble. It skimmed, skipped, danced over the surface. "How about that! Forty feet."

"It was a good toss," Abbey said. "But no way did it travel forty feet."

Travis grinned. "At least forty feet."

Abbey narrowed her eyes, licked her lips, cocked her arm and sidearmed her pebble, giving her wrist a twist at the last moment. "Look at it go! Fifty feet!"

"No way! Forty, maybe."

"You're being deliberately blind."

Travis chuckled. "We're both being deliberately blind. Agreed?"

"Shall we try harder to be objective?"

"Definitely. Yes," Travis said.

Each threw a second pebble, a third.

Those tosses were too close to call. Travis's fourth was long, fifty-five feet, they agreed. When Abbey delivered her fourth pebble, it skimmed, skipped across the water.

"Go!" Abbey yelled. "Go!" In exhorting the pebble, she jumped up and down, splashing herself and Travis. Grinning, she said, "Sorry about that. Sixty feet. It went sixty feet."

"You're not sorry," he said. "Fifty-five, tops."

"Sixty! And a little water on your jeans isn't going to kill you," Abbey teased. "You'll dry sooner or later."

"Oh, yeah?" he said, bending to scoop water into his cupped hands. He splashed her full force.

"Look what you did to my blouse! Now you pay!" Abbey jumped, creating a spray that drenched them both.

"That was dumb. You got yourself as wet as me," Travis observed. "But keep it up and you're going to get *really* wet."

"You wouldn't dare."

Travis grabbed her hand. He inhaled her perfume, the smell of the night. "Last chance, Abbey," he said. "You agreed to be objective—"

"So did you!"

"I was being objective. Now admit that we tied on that last throw or I'll dump you."

"Your problem is that you don't like to lose. You never did," she said, laughing.

Suddenly the game was over for Travis. He dropped her hand and moved toward the bank. "I never minded losing *to* you, Abbey," he said. "I didn't like losing *you*."

Abbey wanted to believe him. She'd believed him when he'd said she owned a place in his heart. So why didn't she believe he hadn't liked losing her?

Because the evidence had been to the contrary.

They didn't speak while drying their feet on the grass and slipping on their shoes. They just could not forget the past, Abbey thought. To be totally honest they had to trust one another, and they didn't. They were stuck in a never-ending game of tactics. Saving face.

"Want to take the shortcut through the pasture?" Travis asked.

"Sure," Abbey agreed.

They crossed to the barbed wire fence. It was slack. Travis shoved the top wire down and held it. Abbey placed her hand on his shoulder to balance herself, then stepped over the wire, smiling up at him as she did.

How he longed for peace between them, Travis found himself thinking. There had been so much good between them, such extraordinary sweetness before they ruined it.

But he knew the trappings of a wrinkled ribbon and jeans would disappear in the morning. In the light of day, this Abbey would slip away, forever, this time. After he refused to yield what she wanted.

They approached the cottonwood where the bull had treed them so long ago. Travis veered toward it, stopping under the branch they'd shared.

"I think that day was the first time I had an inkling that what I felt for you was love," he said, not looking at her.

"We were adolescents," she said. "Incapable of comprehending what real love is."

"You're trying to rationalize what we felt for each other," he said.

"Of course I'm trying to rationalize it."

"It wasn't habit on your part. Or pity on mine," Travis said forcefully. "Call it what it was—love. Because children love, and we loved."

"What we loved were soft, furry kittens and wiggling puppies," she countered.

"Yes. We loved kittens and puppies," he agreed. "And watching robin eggs hatch, fishing in the river, skipping pebbles in the creek."

"And night crawlers. Nice, fat, juicy ones."

"And playing in the cemetery," Travis said.

"We weren't very discriminating when it came to what we loved, were we?" she asked pointedly.

"What I believe is this," he said slowly. "We were more insightful then than we are now. Once we did love, but you weren't happy with it."

He wheeled and jogged toward the farmstead.

Abbey chased after him, his words causing scintillating bliss. She hadn't misjudged his love for her. He had believed he loved her as she'd believed she'd loved him. That made her dependence on him, if not right, at least defensible, because what she'd needed had been his love.

"Why are we running?" she asked, panting.

He stopped, confronted her. "Dammit, Abbey," he said gruffly. "Like it or not, we're the same two people. Making love to you ten years ago was a mistake. Kissing you again would be a grievous mistake. And I'm trying like hell to avoid making it."

"It would be something you'd hate yourself for doing?"

"Yes."

"I'm sick of hearing you say that without saying why you feel that way!"

Anger bolted through Travis, giving him an instant, throbbing headache. She was mauling him emotionally. He was stupid to allow it.

"You're not obtuse," he snapped. "You figure it out."

"I'd never figure you out, not in a million years," she retorted. "But rest easy, Travis. I won't allow you to make the grievous mistake of kissing me. I don't want you to blame me when you wake in the morning hating yourself."

Travis smelled her scent of spring and felt his head spinning. Torn by the pain he heard in her voice, he touched her face. The chill of the night and her anger had left her skin cold.

He rubbed his thumb over her cheekbone. "We're hurting each other," he murmured.

She didn't answer, and there were no night songs to cover the silence, he thought. No crickets harmonizing, no owls hooting. The breeze had gasped its last breath.

What could be heard was the sound of his breathing, rapid and rasping. An explicit statement of his hunger for her, if she was listening.

And he knew she was. He felt her excitement under his fingers. Her body, slightly pressing toward him, was alive. Despite her boast she was responsive, willing.

And there was a feeling of power in knowing at this moment, she wanted him as much as he wanted her.

So why not detach himself emotionally and take what she was willing to give? he reasoned. Why not appease the physical ache? He cupped her head lightly, moved his body to hers, allowing it to indicate his physical desire.

Abbey gasped. She was lost in stirring awareness.

Travis would be the only man who would ever hold her this way. Like it or not, she could search for eons, but never would another man stir such deep-seated need in her.

"Let's talk about the grievous mistake," he said breathlessly. "The one you're going to allow me to make."

He lowered his head, his lips searching for hers.

Abbey drew upon her reservoir of willpower, taking the last of it to say "No."

He took the word from her lips, whispering, "Yes, Abbey. Yes."

His lips toyed with hers. He moistened her lips with the tip of his tongue, probed for acceptance. She started to ascend, soaring on the exquisite bliss, leaving behind the world of complications.

They swayed in place, inches apart. The only contacts between them were his hand lightly cupping her head and their lips. Then not even that. He lifted his lips and the hand, and placed a knuckle under her chin.

She knew he was going to tilt her head back, trail nibbling kisses under her jaw, ending near her ear. But he was taking an agonizingly long time doing it, and she wondered if he'd forgotten how she loved it.

She thought she must have whispered, "Travis, please," because he murmured something unintelligible and began the journey of feathering kisses. By the time his lips were feeling for her pulse, she was beyond demanding explanations for why she wanted Travis to make love to her, beyond caring about reprisals or consequences.

Now all there was was Travis. She would be as close to him as he would allow. Her fingers fumbled for the buttons of his shirt.

The nipples of Abbey's breasts beaded beneath Travis's fingers. Wild urgency caromed about in his mind, then suddenly came into sharp focus. He didn't want Abbey this way. It would be no compensation for the vacuum he'd feel when she left in the morning. The kind of vacuum he'd felt when she left him the first time. One he'd tried to fill with work, women and expensive toys, discovering in them only temporary satisfaction. He was weary of manufacturing joys, planning ways to be happy. He simply wanted to *be* happy.

And Abbey wasn't going to shortchange him this time. He broke off the kiss.

Abbey was slow to comprehend that he was no longer kissing her and that it was she who was seeking his lips. And slower still to comprehend that he was cutting short her quest. Gently but firmly rejecting her.

Shaken, she asked, "Why did you stop?"

"Why continue?" he asked.

"Because you know I want you to make love to me."

"That's the reason," Travis said. "Because you want it." He dropped her hand and pivoted away. "I don't settle for crumbs of affection. Not anymore."

"Crumbs of affection?" Abbey asked dumbly. "You think that's what I was showing you? Crumbs of affection?"

"Was it love, Abbey?" he snapped.

"It wasn't hate."

He nodded, then walked away, leaving Abbey to follow. And follow she did, shedding hot tears of anger and frustration. He didn't notice. She'd have been angry with him if he had. He would have asked why she was crying. How could she explain? She didn't understand herself.

Except that he wasn't predictable. He was driving her crazy without ever half trying or seeming to care.

"Travis. Talk to me."

"What the hell do you want me to say?"

"Nothing!"

Back at the Penny place, Travis opened the car door for her. Abbey straightened her back and marched past him. "I'm not getting in," she said tersely. "When I'm ready to go, I'll walk back into town, thank you."

She crossed the lawn to the front porch, sat down on the steps, looked up at the sky, waiting. He'd come. He wouldn't drive away, leaving her to walk alone through the night. He'd worry that she might get hurt. He'd want to protect her.

He'd come, try to badger her into going with him.

Then, by damn, they'd have it out.

"I'm leaving," he called.

"Drive safely," she called.

She heard him curse, mumble, "Most impossible, most irresponsible and Daniel Hesston must be crazy to trust her."

The door slammed. He strode toward her, a shadow before Abbey could make out his features. He wasn't happy. She wasn't, either.

He stopped, placed his hands on hips as he confronted her. "I could drag you."

"Not your style."

"I could wake Bob and Cassie. Have one of them come back for you."

"You'd have to explain why you were crawling around on their porch roof, and I'd have to explain why I was sitting on the steps out here. It would be embarrassing for them and us," she said. "Don't worry. Go home. I'll be fine."

He heaved a mighty sigh, plopped down beside her. "I can't leave you."

"I know. Now, what was all that about? Crumbs of affection?"

"Let's not get into it."

"I promise you that I'm not going to get angry."

"I've heard that one before," he said, not without humor.

Abbey smiled. "Yes, I think you have. But this time I mean it. We've got to talk this out."

"Why do we have to talk it out?"

"Because it's hurting us. You told me that you didn't want to hurt me anymore. I don't want to hurt you. But if you won't talk to me, that will hurt. So why did you accuse me of giving you crumbs of affection?"

"You said you were thinking about getting married."

It seemed like a million years ago when she'd said that. "Yes. I said it."

"Why?" he asked.

"To keep you from kissing me."

"To keep me from kissing you," he repeated. "But you were willing to make love with me?"

"Yes."

"If we'd made love, what would you have called it, tossing a bridal bouquet to the ex-lover?"

"You didn't make love to me because you think I love someone else?"

Travis started to say yes, but knew he had been lying. He didn't care about Evan. He cared about Abbey, about himself and how she'd managed to hurt him.

The night of their senior prom he'd asked her to marry him. She'd said no, then *allowed* him to make love to her. Afterward he'd felt as if she'd tried to appease him.

"No," he admitted. "I was lying. I'd have made love to you, thinking you might love another man. But it suddenly occurred to me while I was kissing you that you might be *allowing* me to make love to you," Travis said. "Kind of like a gratuity."

"In return for what?"

Travis knew the fury Abbey would rain upon him if he answered honestly. Destruction of the tentative steps they'd taken toward one another was inevitable. But she'd asked. He wasn't going to lie. "For what you want, Abbey. This house. The Penny place."

"And you think I'd prostitute myself to get it?" she asked.

## Chapter Eleven

"My heart tells me no. My mind asks why? Why else would Abbey want to make love with me?"

"Your heart tells the truth," Abbey said. "I don't know when it started, maybe the first day of school when you said, 'There ain't nothin' to be scared of, Abbey. I won't let nothin' hurt you.' But I loved you, and loved you desperately."

When he tried to speak, she quieted him by placing her fingers upon his lips. His lips moved against her fingertips in a gesture as lovingly sweet as what she saw in his eyes. The effect was breathtaking.

But she said what needed to be said. "The key word is desperate, Travis. And a desperate love isn't a love of strength," she said firmly. "It's a love of dependency. It's the kind of love my mother had for my father. If we had married, it wouldn't have worked out."

"I know," Travis said. "You needed independence."

With that they began talking. It was if they'd each kept a daily diary of their lives, Abbey reflected. They didn't rush, flipping the pages and omitting details, but turned the pages leisurely, learning about each other. How they had changed. Or hadn't changed at all.

When it grew chilly, Travis asked whether or not Abbey wanted to call it a night. She shook her head. He slipped his arm around her. Abbey snuggled close.

"Remarkable," Travis whispered into her ear.

"What's remarkable?" Abbey asked.

He kissed her ear. "This—holding you. I don't want to mess it up with anything less meaningful."

"I know what you feel, what you mean," she said.

They talked until dawn flowered the sky with orange and yellow-gold clouds. "We'd better go," Travis said. "You'll need to catch a couple of hours of sleep before heading back to Minneapolis."

"You're still trying to take care of me," Abbey observed easily. "But I don't feel sleepy."

"I don't, either." Travis laughed. "But I will. And you will. So get some rest. I don't want to worry about you falling asleep driving."

Abbey sat up and stretched. "What time is it, anyway?"

Travis glanced at his watch. "A few minutes after six. About the Penny—"

"It isn't eight o'clock yet," Abbey said. Over his shoulder she spotted a baby rabbit coming from the direction of the barn. "Look," she whispered, pointing to where the tiny animal had stopped, ears alert.

When the rabbit sensed it wasn't alone, it turned tail, disappearing under the foundation of the barn. She and Travis had loved baby rabbits. Roy had told them they'd have no problem catching one. All they had to do was put a little table salt in the palms of their hands, sneak up on the rabbit and drop the salt onto the rabbit's tail.

"Both naive on that one, weren't we?" Travis asked.

"Our mistake was in trusting Roy," Abbey said, smiling. "Why do you suppose he told us that?"

"To see how long it would take us to figure out that if we were close enough to dump salt on the rabbit's tail, we were close enough to catch it," Travis said.

"Which was impossible."

"Maybe more like improbable," Travis suggested. "Because yesterday I thought what happened tonight was impossible. But it wasn't."

"When I wrote you all those letters the first year of college, that's what I told myself," Abbey said. "'Why am I writing? It's impossible.' He said nothing would make him happier than never seeing me again."

"I didn't get any letters."

"I didn't send any letters."

"I wasn't lying about thinking about you, Abbey," Travis said. "In fact I got as far as calling you once. The moment your secretary said, 'Ms. Baird's office,' I knew I'd made a mistake. I told her I'd dialed the wrong number."

The silence was long and studied. Abbey wasn't thinking about a compromise on the Penny place. She was thinking that no matter what happened tomorrow morning, she couldn't accept the idea that they'd never see each other *this way* again.

"I suppose you didn't ask to speak to me for the same reason I didn't send the letters," she said. "I was too proud to take the first step—out of fear of being rejected."

"That and when your secretary called you Ms. Baird. It reminded me of all the reasons why you'd left Beaver Crossing," he said. "And boiled down, it came back to one thing. There wasn't room in your life for me, not the way you wanted to live it."

"There was room," Abbey said firmly. "I never dreamed of sharing my life with anyone but you. All I wanted was time. Time to go to college, get my life in order—"

"Abbey, admit it. What I had to offer wasn't enough," Travis said heavily. "The goals Jen set for you were more important to you than any need you had for me."

"Mother didn't have anything to do with us," Abbey protested.

"You said it yourself, Abbey. She wanted you to do better than she had," he said. "She pounded it home. Family name. Penny pride. She lived vicariously through you."

Abbey shook her head in denial.

Travis stood, hovered over her. "Then why didn't you say, 'I can't marry you now, but I will marry you someday'? You could have said that. But you didn't."

"I didn't because I didn't trust what you felt for me," Abbey said. "I thought all you wanted from me was a physical relationship."

Travis's laugh was short, gently scoffing. "After all those years of self-control? How could you suddenly decide all I wanted was sex?"

He extended his hand, pulled Abbey to a standing position.

"The first time we made love," Abbey said, "I was the one who pushed it."

"I know. Your father had died," he said. "You were feeling alone."

"I wasn't alone," Abbey said. "I had you. But we were literally headed in different directions. You were going to Arizona, I was going to the University of Iowa."

"We'd been headed in different directions with our lives a long time before that, Abbey," he said. "You could have gone to Arizona. I could have gone to your university. We could have been together, but you didn't want it that way."

"I know," Abbey agreed. "I had this idea that I needed to test myself, see if I could make it without you always being there to tell me that I could. But that night I was so afraid of losing you. I needed you to hold me, assure me. That's why I asked you to make love to me. But you said no, that you'd hate yourself if you did. Yet after the first night, it seemed to me that was all you had on your mind."

"You think your love for me was desperate," Travis said. He touched her forehead with his finger, flicked her bangs, stepped away. "Let me tell you about desperate love. After the first time we made love, we promised it wouldn't happen again, that we'd control our emotions. But I was lying. I knew we would make love, because I wanted you pregnant."

"I can't believe that," Abbey said. "That day outside Irene's you talked about not being obligated—"

"Believe it," he said. "It was the only way I could think of keeping you from leaving me. But when I realized what I was doing, trying to physically tie you to me, I knew I had to let you go. That's why I said that."

"You loved me enough to drive me out of your life," Abbey said, her voice trembling in wonder.

"Ah, Abbey, I wish that had been so, but it wasn't. I was trying to save face. Trying to show you that I didn't need you in my life any more than you needed me in your life. Hate me now?"

Abbey smiled, slipped her hand into his as they strolled toward the car. "I don't hate you. Do you love me?"

Travis stalled, swinging her around until she half lay against his hip. He looked down into her eyes. "That's a hell of a switch in topic."

"It is a switch. Do you?"

"I love who you were."

"Could you love who I am?"

"Didn't you tell me that you plan on being a vice president of Hesston someday?"

"I did and I do," Abbey said.

"There's no room for a man like me in the life of a woman who will be the vice president of the Hesston chain," Travis said. "You know that. I know that."

"You're shoving me out of your life again, aren't you?"

"Look at me, Abbey. What do you see?"

"Someone who understands me—"

"No. What you see is Beaver Crossing. Beaver Crossing, Abbey! That's what I am."

"I love Beaver Crossing," Abbey insisted.

"I know," Travis said sadly. "I know you do, but something makes you fight to escape it. More to the point, me. So the answer to 'could I love you' has to be that maybe I could. But I will not allow myself to love you, Abbey."

"If you feel that way, then what was tonight about?" Abbey demanded.

"It was about trying to recapture the feeling of spontaneous joy, about spending a few hours with my friend." He glanced at his watch, but not before Abbey had seen the sadness that matched her own. "Is it eight?" she asked.

"Another hour."

"I need you to be my friend," she said, feeling panicky. "I need to know when I leave that I can look forward to seeing you again. I can't stand the idea of having to avoid you."

"You are asking the truly impossible now," Travis said heavily. "I can't be that kind of friend to you again, because to me being your friend and loving you are synonymous."

"Are we going back to avoiding each other?" she asked.

"It would be easier on both of us if we did."

Abbey knew her heart was breaking. She felt the twist, the stab. But maybe he was right. They had come this far, mended a few old wounds without making new ones.

"I was being unfair in trying to push you into an immediate decision about the buildings," she said. "Why don't you think it over and call me? We'll talk about it then."

"A couple of days," Travis said. "I'll call."

"Promise?"

"Yes. I promise."

Thank God, Abbey thought. He hadn't closed the door on her yet. Not yet.

With all that had changed for Abbey over the weekend, she was surprised when she walked into her office the following Monday morning to discover nothing there had changed.

She was settled behind her desk and starting to work, when Nicole swept into the room, notepad in hand. "Still having lunch with Daniel?" she asked.

"Is it on the schedule?"

"Don't snap at me," Nicole snapped. "You're the one who keeps changing your schedule. All I do is try to keep up with you." She tapped the point of her pen on the notepad.

"Did I snap?" Abbey asked.

Nicole mimicked the tone of voice Abbey had used. "Is that snap? Or is that snap?"

"It was definitely snippy, if not snappy," Abbey admitted. "I'm sorry. No excuse, I know, but when I'm tired, I'm grumpy. And Saturday night I never went to bed."

Nicole lowered her pad, holding it at waist level, and raised a brow. "Never went to bed?"

"An...old friend and I were talking," Abbey said. "If I'm scheduled with Daniel for lunch today. I still am."

"Back up to where you said, 'An...old friend,'" Nicole said. "Male or female old friend?"

"Male," Abbey said. She picked up the papers she'd been looking through. The print blurred.

She had slept several hours Sunday morning, before going with Cassie and Bob to the farm. They'd hauled a load of junk to the landfill. There was at least another load of junk for the landfill, but it was getting late, so they'd loaded five pieces of furniture Bob and Cassie wanted to use and had returned to town.

By the time they'd eaten lunch and Abbey had stopped at the cemetery to visit her parents' graves, it was time to leave Beaver Crossing. She had been so exhausted when she reached her apartment, all she could think of was getting to bed. She hadn't even unloaded the china.

She'd stumbled into her bedroom, tossed her clothing aside, taken the shortest bath in history—at least she thought she'd bathed—fumbled into her nightie and fallen onto the bed.

But the moment she hit the mattress, it was as if the caffeine of ten cups of coffee hit her. She'd been wide-awake and had lain for hours thinking about Travis, the memories they had made in the hours they'd been together.

"What are you doing?" Nicole asked.

Abbey jerked to attention, looked at the papers she was holding. "Ah...the inventory sheets from the Lincoln store don't seem to be here."

"You didn't ask for them, so they aren't there," Nicole said. "This friend must be some kind of guy if you can't keep your mind on your work."

Abbey laughed. "Know what? I'm too blasted tired to try to convince you otherwise. He is some kind of guy and his name is Travis."

"You're in love with him," Nicole stated.

Abbey briefly described her friendship with Travis. "I loved him once. I think I still love him."

"I'm no expert on the subject, but if looks do tell, your expression tells me that you love him," Nicole observed.

"Love . . . isn't always enough," Abbey said slowly. "At least, it has never been with Travis and me. The differences that caused us to go in different directions with our lives still exist."

"You'll work it out if you want to work it out," Nicole said. "I'll get the Lincoln inventory."

Work it out. Work it out. Travis's life was in Beaver Crossing. Her life was here. Sights set on the vice president's office. Human nature being what it was, there would be times when she would wonder about Travis and miss him.

Because among the things she'd learned over the weekend was the undeniable fact that there was something viable and tangible in her relationship with Travis. Something she didn't fully understand, couldn't describe. But she felt the uniqueness of it and knew that she would never feel it with any other man.

Nicole came into the office and slipped the Lincoln invoice onto the desk. Abbey forced her attention to the work at hand. She dutifully stuck to it for an hour.

The buzzer on the intercom sounded. Abbey flipped the switch. "Evan's on line three," Nicole said.

"Put him through," Abbey said.

After they'd greeted each other, Evan asked, "How did your weekend go?"

"Quite nicely," Abbey said.

"I missed you," Evan said, paused, then asked, "Are you free for dinner tonight?"

Abbey was about to say no, but she respected Evan too much to play a cat-and-mouse game. She knew he wanted commitment. She knew she would be wrong to encourage him. She didn't love him, and never would love him the way he deserved to be loved.

She was going to tell him that, but not over the telephone. That would be unkind and cowardly.

"I've had a busy day and really don't feel up to going out," she said. "What if I stop for some chicken and salad? We can eat at my place, say around seven."

"Sounds good to me," Evan said.

By four, Abbey had cleared her desk of priority work. She had also been in on a telephone conference Daniel had held with two managers. And had been bored out of her bean listening.

She was considering leaving early. That way, she'd have time to pick up the food and unload the china before Evan arrived. While they ate, she'd tell him what she had to say and hope he understood.

The intercom buzzed. She knew it. She'd waited too long to leave. Now Daniel was on the line with some last-minute problem that needed her immediate attention.

"What now?" Abbey asked Nicole.

"This is going to put zip in your day," Nicole said. "I've got Travis Matthews on hold. And lordy, lordy, what a voice! Tall, blond and brown-eyed, with a build of a surfer?"

"Six feet. Dark-haired and blue-eyed. And physically... pleasing. Put him through."

"Is now the time to ask for a raise?" Nicole teased.

"Now is the time you could get canned."

Nicole laughed outright.

Abbey's hand was shaking as she reached for the phone. She made a fist with her fingers, then stretched them. Once, twice, to ease the tension. She picked up the handset, punched the blinking button.

"Hello, Travis," she said.

"Hello, Abbey," he said.

Her breath caught. A little more than a day since she'd heard his voice, and already she missed him so much. How could that be? One weekend after ten years of separation. "Have a busy day?" she asked. "Did the auger stay fixed?"

"It stayed fixed. Otherwise I'm not sure how the day did go. I think I slept through it," he said. "Guess I'm too old to miss a night's sleep and not pay for it."

Abbey swung her chair around to look out the window. "Me, too. I've been grouchy all day."

"I can believe that. You were always grouchy when you were tired. Abbey," he said, "why I called. I'm going to do another survey on the rock I have available."

"Maybe I placed too much importance—"

"I'm talking compromise, Abbey," Travis said. "If I can find a way to supply the rock and leave the house standing, I will. I wanted you to know."

Abbey's head reeled. "Thank you, Travis."

"You're welcome, Abbey."

"Ah, maybe you'd like my home number," Abbey said. "It's unlisted. In case something comes up."

"Good idea," he said. "Never can tell when something might come up."

"Have a pencil handy?"

"Dangling over the paper."


Evan arrived early, having driven straight from his office. Abbey was just carrying the last box of dishes inside.

Even took it from her and followed her into the apartment. When they reached the dining room, she said, "Just set it in the corner with the rest of the boxes."

"No china cabinet yet, I see," Evan said.

"It's not here, but I have one," Abbey said. She told him about Clara's offer of the china cabinet and bedroom furniture.

"I thought you'd go with something more modern in this apartment," Evan observed offhand. "Chrome. White and black. The possibilities are limitless."

Abbey laughed. "A change in location doesn't mean a change in taste. Me with a black and white theme?"

Evan laughed. "Okay. I was thinking about myself."

Abbey ignored the hint. They ate in the kitchen. Evan was accustomed to a more formal atmosphere, but he made himself comfortable. Abbey wasn't comfortable. She kept trying to think of a way to get into what she had to say. They were having after-dinner coffee and she was still searching for the right words.

"I'm beginning to get the feeling you've got something on your mind," Evan said.

"Have there been many moments when I've stared into space?" she asked.

"Quite a few," Evan said. "Not to mention the lengthy silences, failure to answer questions."

"I do have something on my mind."

"I've never known you not to speak your mind. What's the problem? Me? Something I've done?"

Abbey rose, stepped to the coffeepot, came back and refilled their cups. "Me," she said. "The problem is me."

"I don't know if I like the sound of this," Evan said.

"I care for you—"

"Caring is good," Evan said easily. "I'm the kind of man who can be happy with caring. Marry me. We'll work on making you fall in love with me."

Abbey smiled. "I have a friend who suggested that I work to fall in love with you. And I think I might have tried it, if I didn't believe I was in love with someone else."

"Since when?" Evan asked.

"Since forever," Abbey said. "And it would be unfair for me to allow you to think there might be a chance for us. That's what I wanted to tell you tonight."

"What brought this on?" Evan asked.

Evan deserved to be told, so Abbey told him.

"Maybe I'm blind," Evan said when she'd finished talking. "Or maybe I'm a fool, but I have to ask the obvious question. If you love him, what's the problem?"

"He doesn't want to reestablish our relationship because he sees no future for us," Abbey said. "And I'm not sure there is, either. All I know is that I couldn't stand failing with him again."

The telephone rang. "Excuse me," Abbey said. "It's probably Daniel." She thought about answering in the den, but decided to take the call in the kitchen.

She reached for the phone with her left hand, and a pad and pencil with her right. When Daniel called, he always came at her with rapid-fire information.

"Baird residence," she said.

"You said to call in case something came up."

"Travis! What's come up?" She started to doodle.

"I was watching some show on television and reading a novel and couldn't concentrate on either. Do you have time to visit?"

Abbey grimaced. "I do have company. Ah..." Blast it, she couldn't lie. She worked the pencil furiously. "Evan's here."

"Then I won't keep you," Travis said.

She couldn't peg what she heard in his voice. Sudden disillusionment? Distrust? "I'll call you—"

"No problem. I'll catch you later. Good night, Abbey."

Abbey returned the phone to the cradle and looked at her doodling. She'd written the word Travis and drawn a heart around it. It had been years since she'd done something like that.

"Bad news?" Evan asked.

"No. I don't think so," Abbey said, trying to smile. "But then with Travis, I never know."

* * *

He'd done a lot of foolish things in his life, Travis thought. Calling Abbey at home had been the most foolish. No! Admitting he'd called to visit had been the most foolish. Now she knew damn well he'd been thinking about her.

Maybe not. She might think he'd called to discuss the Penny place. He'd told her they didn't have a future, and they didn't. So his credibility might still be intact with her. But not with himself.

If he valued his pride so highly, why had he given in to the impulse to call her? He was weak. That was what he was. He missed her. He'd wanted to talk to her, hear her laugh, hear her say anything...anything but, "Evan's here."

He felt more sinner than saint. He couldn't think of anyone who deserved happiness more than Abbey. If she could find happiness with Evan, he should be happy for her.

But he wasn't. He grabbed a beer, switched on the answering machine and walked outside. He wandered away from the house, found a log and sat, popping the can.

By the time he finished the beer, he'd decided what he needed was companionship. He looked to the sky. The moon wasn't quite as bright as when he and Abbey had skipped pebbles. He should have dumped her, just for the fun they would have gotten from it.

Life without Abbey? It wasn't something he wanted to dwell on. He wasn't going to dwell on it.

Abbey was back at the phone. Evan's leave-taking had been quick. There were no hard feelings between them, only understanding and the promise of continued friendship. He'd call.

Abbey barely remembered saying goodbye. All she had on her mind was getting to the telephone, calling Travis.

The phone rang five times, then the answering machine clicked in, delivering the message that he would be gone for a couple of hours. She hated answering machines.

Nevertheless, at the beep of the tone she said, "Travis. This is Abbey. Call when you have time."

She waited three hours and grew annoyed. She berated him for calling earlier, piquing her curiosity. Had he called about the Penny place? Or had he simply called because he wanted to talk to her?

At eleven she gave up waiting.

She showered, slipped into her nightie and collapsed onto the bed, falling asleep immediately. The moment the alarm rang the next morning, she was thinking about Travis, wondering why he hadn't returned her call.

Throughout the day, each time Nicole notified her of an incoming call, her heart raced in anticipation, until she heard it wasn't Travis.

That evening she stood in the dining room, staring at the spot on the wall where the china cabinet would go. She wondered if she shouldn't rent a van this weekend and drive back to Beaver Crossing.

The dining room would certainly look more homey with Clara's china cabinet standing against the wall, her mother's table in the center of the room....

Could Travis be right? she wondered. Had her mother lived her life vicariously through her? Had she

left Beaver Crossing because she'd wanted to leave, or
because her mother had planted in her mind the idea
that she had to leave to make something of herself?

She made herself a sandwich and sat down at the
table, eating it—and staring at the telephone. Maybe
Travis's answering machine was on the blink. Answering machines could do weird things.

What the heck. She moved to the phone, dialed his
number and got his answering machine. At the sound
of the beep, she said, "Travis, this is Abbey. Did you
call last night because something had come up with the
Penny place?"

She was about to hang up when his voice came on
the line, sounding so dear, so welcome. "Hello, Abbey. Nothing new with the Penny place yet. What have
you been doing?"

She told him.

## Chapter Twelve

They talked three hours.

Abbey learned there was a For Sale sign in front of the Markroy mansion. Clara and Tom were asking forty thousand. Both agreed it was a steal, if anyone was in the market for a twelve-room mansion located in a small town.

"There's a possibility someone will buy it and turn it into an apartment house," Travis said.

"I wouldn't like to see that happen," Abbey said.

"Nor would I," he agreed. "But I'm inclined to believe that's what will happen."

The next night he called her. He was still waiting for the reports on the survey, he told her. Since they hadn't talked about Evan the night before, Abbey brought up Evan's name, telling Travis that she wouldn't be dating Evan again, even though he was a wonderful person.

Travis made no comment. But Abbey hadn't expected he would. She'd only wanted him to know.

He told her that he'd transplanted lilac shoots from the Penny place to his place. He'd also transplanted asters and mums. Abbey didn't know whether her delight stemmed from what he was saying, or from the sweet sound of his voice. All she knew was the next best thing to being with Travis was talking to him. And they did that for four hours.

She called him on Wednesday night. He'd gotten the survey back and had talked with Roy. "Dad reminded me that to him a verbal agreement is as binding as a written contract. He said when he promised Jen, he knew she'd never live to see the place back in her hands and that he always knew you'd be the one to claim it," Travis said. "He thinks sixty thousand for the house and the acre it occupies is reasonable."

"It isn't reasonable. It's giving me the house," Abbey said.

"You'll have to fight Dad on this one, Abbey." Travis laughed. "He says if I try to hold you up for anything more or if you get bullheaded about it, we'll both be in trouble with him."

Abbey chuckled. "All right. Sixty thousand. Now what did your survey tell you?" she asked.

"I'm going to be short five to ten acres," Travis said. "I'm looking for a subcontractor. It shouldn't be too difficult to arrange."

"But you'll lose money on the deal, won't you?"

"You know too much about the running of a business for me to try to lie," Travis said. "We'll lose money."

"You're selling me one acre," Abbey said, pausing to do some quick, mental calculating. "You have to provide access to the house and the lane is a good two blocks long. How many acres are you really losing by selling me one acre?"

"It doesn't matter," Travis said. "I'd still be short."

"It matters to me," Abbey said. "How many?"

"An estimated five."

"We can't do that—"

"The only alternative would be for me to dig the pit around the house and give you access by boat," Travis said.

"Ha to that idea," Abbey said. "But isn't there anything else we can do? Access from another direction, from your folks' lane, maybe?"

"We'll think about it," Travis said.

They talked for three hours and after they'd said goodbye, an idea Abbey had been mulling around began to take shape.

On Thursday night they talked for four hours about nothing important, which was why it was significant. By the end of the conversation, Abbey knew exactly what she had to do.

The moment Abbey walked into the office on Friday morning, Nicole greeted her with, "Thank goodness you're here. Mr. Hesston has already called down twice. He wants to see you like ten minutes ago."

Abbey glanced at the clock, set her purse and briefcase on Nicole's desk. "It isn't even nine," she said. "What's on his mind?"

"All he said was that he'd tried to call you last night and your line was busy. Anybody I know?"

"Travis."

"I tried to call you Wednesday night," Nicole said. "Your line was busy. Travis?"

"Travis. We've had a lot of business to conduct."

"Business," Nicole said. "Okay. I'll buy that, but wouldn't it be cheaper to drive back and forth?"

"Or fly," Abbey said, distracted. "Which I'm going to do tomorrow morning. Fly to Beaver Crossing."

"I thought you were going to rent a van to bring back some furniture," Nicole said.

"I changed my mind," Abbey said.

"You don't like to fly," Nicole stated.

"I know I don't like to fly," Abbey said, half laughing. "But do me a favor, will you, please? Check to see what flight I can get into Sioux City in the morning. I'll go up to see what Daniel wants."

Nicole bent her head, mumbling.

"I didn't hear what you said."

Nicole looked up. "I said, 'Why pay for a ticket?' You're already flying."

Smiling, Abbey headed for the door. The phone rang. Abbey paused in the doorway, waiting to see whether or not it was for her. "Yes, Mr. Hesston, she's arrived," Nicole said. She pointed her finger at Abbey and mouthed *go*. Abbey stepped into the hall. "She's on her way up, Mr. Hesston."

Abbey smiled at Daniel's secretary, a woman in her early sixties, then glanced through the open door. She could see the top of Daniel's bald head as he bent over his desk.

"Daniel is expecting me, Mildred," Abbey said in a voice loud enough for Daniel to hear.

"Well, aren't you the lucky one," Mildred said.

"He's in one of his lovable moods, I presume." Abbey glanced into Daniel's office again. His head had come up several inches, just enough so that she knew he was listening.

"As lovable as he gets," Mildred said.

"I heard that," Daniel said. "Abbey, would you stop encouraging Mildred's insubordination and get in here?"

Abbey stepped into the office, closing the door behind her. Daniel straightened, pushed away from the desk. "Did you take your telephone off the hook last night?" he asked.

Daniel's office was austere, and the chairs, save for the one he occupied, didn't encourage idle visiting.

Abbey walked to the straight-backed chair closest to the desk and sat down. "Daniel," she said firmly, "I have enjoyed working for you. You know that, don't you?"

"So you've said. What's that got to do with anything?" Daniel asked.

His halfhearted attempt to intimidate Abbey failed. "In plain words, you don't own every minute of my day."

The leather of Daniel's chair wheezed when he shifted his heavy body. "You've never objected, complained—"

"I know I haven't," Abbey said. "But until this past week, I didn't know why I didn't complain. It's a long story, Daniel. Suffice it to say I grew up in a dysfunctional family and developed a nearly unhealthy need to try to please those I cared about. I care about you. I wanted your approval, so I allowed you to make unjustified claims on my time.

"Was it an emergency last night?" she asked. When Daniel shook his head, she said, "Then you have no right to act out of sorts about not being able to reach me, because I do have the right to talk to whomever I please."

"It's a man!" Daniel said.

"His name is Travis," Abbey said. "He tells me that he always knew I had soul, that I was singularly remarkable, that he has always respected me and approved of me, and that I had nothing to prove to him. How about that, Daniel?"

"I've told you that you're remarkable," Daniel grumbled. "Look at the position you have."

"As a matter of fact, you have *never* told me," Abbey said. "I do appreciate hearing it now, but to be honest, it isn't as important to me as it once would have been, because I feel very good about who I am right now."

Daniel pushed back in the chair. "Don't tell me you're going to do something foolish like getting married," he grumbled.

Abbey ignored his grumbling. "Why were you trying to reach me last night?"

"I had last week's purchase orders at home and I was looking them over," Daniel said. "I saw where you'd boosted the inventory on Bella Sports. The line is untested—"

"Did you compare the February sales with the March sales?"

"No," Daniel admitted. "I didn't have that data on hand. I'll have Mildred bring the reports in."

Fifteen minutes later Daniel looked up. "The percentage of sales with Bella Sports is impressive," he said. "But it's a small test of buyer preference. I don't know that the line deserves the kind of confidence you placed in it."

"It's a matter of opinion," Abbey said. "I have a gut feeling, Daniel. Bella Sports is going to stay hot."

"You know how I feel about that kind of talk."

Abbey laughed. "Sometimes you just have to go with gut feeling," she said, thinking of Travis. "Yes. Sometimes you have to do that, because that's all there is, the feeling that it *is* right."

She stood. "Daniel," she said slowly, "I'm flying to Beaver Crossing tomorrow morning, so I'll be out of town this weekend."

"According to you, you don't have to have my permission."

"I wasn't asking for permission," she said. "You know I appreciate all you've done for me, don't you, Daniel?"

"Now, what are you going to tell me that I'm not going to like hearing?"

"I'm giving you two weeks' notice—"

"You are getting married!"

"At this moment I don't know. What I do know is that the person I am and the person I want to be belongs in Beaver Crossing. So I'm going home," Abbey said. "Do you want my resignation in writing?"

"Henry retires in two years," Daniel said contemplatively. "If I promised you his vice presidency, would you consider staying?"

"I'd be tempted," Abbey said.

"But only tempted," Daniel said.

"Only tempted."

"What in the blue devil can Beaver Crossing offer you?" Daniel asked.

"What it can offer is the peace of mind I've never had," Abbey said. "And the chance to make my long-held dream of owning a small clothing shop come true."

"So you're going to be my competition?" Daniel asked, eyes twinkling.

"In my opinion, no one can compete with you," Abbey said sincerely.

"I'd wish you luck, but I don't want you to leave me."

"Would you wish me happiness?" Abbey asked.

"You've got me there," Daniel said, smiling. "I wish you happiness."

"Thank you, Daniel," Abbey said.

"Get back to work," Daniel said. "You're on my time!"

Abbey was chuckling when she walked past Mildred. "You're right. Loveable as can be."

When Travis called that night, Abbey stopped packing her overnight case to answer the phone. He informed her straightaway that a crew was going to the Penny place in the morning to begin razing the barn.

He heard her take a deep breath. "I know how you feel."

"I know you do," Abbey said.

He didn't mention the house. Abbey didn't bring the subject up. Nor did she tell him about her conversation with Daniel or that she'd decided to deliver the check for the Penny place in person.

"I suppose you'll supervise the crew," she said.

"I'll go over in the morning to check things out," he said. "I want to make sure the foreman of the crew understands I want as much as possible of the barn siding salvaged."

A short time later they said goodbye. Abbey glanced at the clock. It was almost ten. Her plane left at eight in the morning, arrived at Sioux Gateway a little after nine. She could be back in Beaver Crossing with Travis by ten. But could she possibly last twelve hours?

She had missed him before, feeling despair and helplessness. She missed him now, feeling joy and anticipation. Her search for love was taking her home.

At exactly twenty after nine, Abbey pitched her overnight case onto the passenger seat of the small sedan she'd rented at the Sioux Gateway airport. At ten to ten she turned into the lane of the Penny place.

Rain had been predicted, but the sky was blue. Like the color of Travis's eyes. She laughed. Now she could enjoy their riveting quality. She wouldn't have to guard against susceptibility or vulnerability anymore. She trusted Travis.

Half a dozen pickups were parked at the farmstead, Travis's among them. Men in yellow hard hats were working on the barn, most with crowbars and hammers. But she didn't see Travis.

Abbey parked the car near the house, away from the flow of activity, then stood for a long time, painstakingly studying the house. The sun was treating the house kindly, brushing shadows over the blemishes. She locked the details of how the house looked into her memory.

She had packed her camera. Later she would take pictures of the farmstead, but first things first. She approached a young man carrying pieces of barn siding, waiting until he'd added them to a growing stack before saying, "I'm looking for Travis Matthews. Is he inside the barn?"

"Mr. Matthews? He was around," the young man said. He glanced over his shoulder, called to a second young man who was using a crowbar to loosen siding. "Hey, Will! You know where Mr. Matthews is?"

"He said something about checking a vein of gravel," Will said. He gestured toward the pasture. "The last time I saw him, he was headed toward the river."

Abbey thanked the young man and walked to the pasture gate. She was wearing jeans, a red jersey blouse. After she'd talked with Travis, she was going to attack the shed with real determination and finish the job.

Before reaching the Big Sioux River, on impulse she swung right and passed the cottonwood tree. She found Travis standing in the creek, tossing pebbles. She watched him until he felt her presence and turned toward her, smiling. Her heart hammered. Her breathing was shallow. Travis was love.

Travis wondered if his yearning for Abbey had been so powerful that he'd called up a vision of her. "Hello, Abbey."

"Hello, Travis."

"Come to play?"

She nodded, knelt and removed her tennis shoes. Her hair fell over her shoulders, gently caressing her breasts. She rolled up the jeans legs to her knees, then waded into the water to join him.

To tranquilize the urgent demands of his body, Travis bent, picked up a pebble and handed it to her. "I'm glad it was you and not one of the men who caught me wading," he said.

"I'll never squeal on you," Abbey said. "Our secret, that you've got a kid streak in you."

"Promise?" Travis asked.

"Double promise."

Travis let fly with a pebble. "Neat toss, if I do say so myself."

Abbey let fly. She trilled, "Look at it go! I beat you again!"

"You're stretching it."

Abbey turned, gazed up into Travis's eyes. She'd intended to approach him slowly, lead into what she was thinking in a methodical, reasonable manner, allow him time to gather his thoughts and respond. But her need to touch him was compelling. She stepped close, placed her hands on his waist.

"You're a sore loser, Travis Matthews," she said.

"I never minded losing to you, Abbey Baird."

Abbey slipped her fingers through the belt loops, and using them as leverage, lifted herself up until their lips met. She greeted him with a light kiss.

"Isn't there more to that thought?" she asked urgently. "Something like you didn't like losing me?"

"Gospel," Travis said.

"You were annihilated," she murmured. "You wondered if living had always been so lonely, and if you'd always feel so empty inside."

"I was annihilated. Life was empty of emotion, without direction," he whispered, reaching for her hair and brushing the ends over his lips. "How did you know?"

"Because I felt it, lived through it as you did," Abbey said. "But no more."

She eased her fingers from the loops, stepped away, slipped her hand into her pocket and brought out a check, written in the amount of sixty thousand dollars. She handed it to Travis.

"It's done," Abbey said. "The promise to my mother is fulfilled. The Penny house is back in Penny hands."

Old fears taunted Travis. She'd gotten what she wanted. Now she'd be gone. "It's done," he agreed.

"Give me the check back," Abbey said. When he frowned, she repeated her request. He handed her the check. She tore it into small pieces, which fluttered to the water and floated away.

"What the devil does this mean?" Travis asked.

"Let's sit on the bank. We'll talk," Abbey suggested. "And I'll try to explain."

A moment later they'd settled on the bromegrass, turned to face each other knee to knee and eye to eye, pulling their legs up, wrapping arms around them.

Once they were in their talking-things-through position, Abbey said, "The house is like a grand old lady. One who has sheltered and nurtured generations of Pennys. But she's tired. She's been abused. I can't justify trying to bring her out of retirement. Raze the house with the rest of the buildings."

"I don't understand."

"I've spent this past week doing some hard thinking about myself," Abbey said. "I was being foolish, Travis, hanging on to that last bit of false pride. I don't need the house to confirm who I am, what worth I have as a person. What the Penny place meant to me as a home is stored up here—" she tapped her head "—in my bank of memories."

"Give it more consideration, Abbey," Travis said. "It would be a good two weeks before the crew finishes with the barn and outbuildings. You might change your mind."

"I won't change my mind. I want you to know *exactly* what is important to me," she said adamantly. "It isn't a house, land or a family name. What is important to me is how I feel about myself and how you feel about me. I'm quitting Daniel and moving back to Beaver Crossing."

In the quiet a blue jay sassed from a nearby tree. There was the muffled roar of motorized activity coming from the pit, and the distant sound of voices.

Travis felt his heart pulsating in his throat. He was afraid to dream, afraid to trust what he saw in her expression. And still fearful that life here with him couldn't live up to what she expected.

"This sounds like an impulsive idea to me," he said. "You've worked hard to get where you are. You deserve to enjoy the rewards that go with it."

"This isn't an impulsive decision," Abbey said. "I'm coming back to Beaver Crossing and I'm staying."

"In a month you'll be bored out of your skull. It won't work."

Abbey rubbed her fingers over his hand, laced her fingers with his, felt the mystic kinship. "I talked to Clara and Tom yesterday. I told them I wanted to buy the mansion."

"The mansion," Travis said. "The mansion?"

She squeezed his fingers. "Just think of the possibilities!"

"I know you won't turn it into an apartment building," he said. "But I can't guess what possibilities you're talking about."

"I'm going to have my own clothes store. I'll call it Country Flair. I'll start small, with a few select lines, and I'll have time to design my own line. I can hardly wait to set up a sewing room. I can't remember the last time I was able to sew to my heart's content."

While he pondered her words, she moved to sit next to him, then slipped an arm around his waist. He responded by tugging her to him.

He sighed. "Abbey, all I've ever wanted was for you to be happy, but coming back to Beaver Crossing . . . I don't know."

"Happiness is the memory we're making now together," she murmured against his cheek. "Happiness will be in all the memories we'll make in the future. Don't try to drive me away because you think it's best for me. Don't deny me the chance for you to fall in love with me again."

Travis pulled her closer. He rested his cheek against the softness of her hair. "I don't want to deny you anything."

She kissed him. "I understand why you don't trust me," Abbey said. "But if you're willing to work on it with me . . ."

"You're pretty confident, aren't you?" Travis asked. "You think I'm a goner."

Abbey smiled serenely, touching his cheek, his jaw possessively. "You know how I am when I want something," she said. "I go after it."

# *Epilogue*

Travis thought he'd been listening for the sound of Abbey's car in the driveway. So when he turned from the stove after checking the simmering soup and found her standing in the kitchen door, watching him, he half laughed in embarrassment. He'd been the one with the surprises in mind.

"How long have you been there?" he asked.

"Not long," Abbey said, smiling.

"You could have said hello, cleared your throat," Travis teased.

"I like looking at you," Abbey said. "Is there a law against that?"

She was wearing a floral-patterned dress. Yellow, red, pink and white flowers floated on a darker background. It was her design, one of a few she planned to sell in The Country Flair when it opened for business two weeks from next Monday. Had three months really passed since she'd moved back to Beaver Crossing?

Her hair was brushed back, tied with a dark ribbon matching the background of her dress. Her perfume had the scent of a bouquet of mixed flowers.

"And I like looking at you," he said. "You look as if you're in the mood for romance."

Abbey moved across the room into his waiting arms. "Wasn't that the message you gave me?" she asked. She kissed his chin. "When you came by the shop and suggested dinner at your place? Weren't you saying, 'Come with romance in mind'?"

They kissed easily, soundly. Travis nibbled her lips, caressed her arms. "You got the message right."

He released her, then stepped back to the stove to stir the soup. "We're having vegetable soup, cheese and crackers. And the soup is ready. Mind getting me the serving bowl in the middle of the dining-room table?"

Abbey walked across the kitchen toward the dining area. When she reached the table, she stopped. "Oh, my goodness, Travis! Mother's bowl! I thought when you helped me clean out the shed, I asked you to take it to the landfill, because I was done clinging to the past."

By the time Travis reached her, Abbey was holding the bowl, examining it. "I don't know why I didn't junk it," he said. "Because at the time I was thinking Jen had been right—once something is broken, even mended it's never as strong as it was."

"But you did save the bowl, and mended the two pieces so the seam doesn't show."

Travis nodded. "And I learned that in the mending the bowl became stronger than it was before it was broken. It will contain all the steaming soup we will ever put in it."

"Are you sure?" Abbey asked.

"Very sure," Travis said. "The secret is a magical glue. Like you and me, Abbey."

"You're proposing?"

"You excite me. You challenge me. You devil me. You belong in the house I built for you. I think that might be what I'm doing," Travis teased lovingly.

Abbey noted the smile deep in his eyes, the one telling her that he had another surprise in reserve. "Think?" she asked.

"Set the bowl back on the table, then slip your fingers into my right jeans pocket," he said.

Abbey did as he ordered, felt a ring and pulled it out. She laid the wedding band, two slender links of gold woven together, in the palm of her hand.

She was so affected by the beauty of the ring and Travis's declaration that their relationship had been mended and was stronger than ever, that all she could do was look at him.

"It was my Grandmother Brownlee's wedding ring," Travis said. "Before she died, she gave the ring to me, telling me to give it to the woman I loved most in the world. I was twelve years old at the time.

"I had the ring with me ten years ago, when I first asked you to marry me, because you were the woman I loved," Travis said. "You are the woman I love. My dear, best friend forever, will you marry me?"

Tears blurred Abbey's vision. "My dear, best friend forever, yes." She handed the ring to Travis. "Please, put the ring where it belongs."

He took her left hand, slipped the ring onto her finger, raised her hand to his lips and kissed the finger wearing the band.

"Welcome home, Abbey."

* * * * *

## WRITTEN IN THE STARS

**Star-crossed lovers?**
**Or a match made in heaven?**

Why are some heroes strong and silent ... and others charming and cheerful? The answer is WRITTEN IN THE STARS!

Coming each month in 1991, Silhouette Romance presents you with a special love story written by one of your favorite authors—highlighting the hero's astrological sign! From January's sensible Capricorn to December's disarming Sagittarius, you'll meet a dozen dazzling and distinct heroes.

Twelve heavenly heroes ... twelve wonderful Silhouette Romances destined to delight you. Look for one WRITTEN IN THE STARS title every month throughout 1991—only from Silhouette Romance.

STAR

*Silhouette Books*®

proudly presents
the long-awaited "prequel" volume of

## LOVE AND GLORY

★

by
### LINDSAY McKENNA

### *Dawn of Valor*

In the summer of '89, Silhouette Special Edition premiered three novels celebrating America's men and women in uniform: LOVE AND GLORY, by bestselling author Lindsay McKenna. Featured were the proud Trayherns, a military family as bold and patriotic as the American flag—three siblings valiantly battling the threat of dishonor, determined to triumph . . . in love and glory.

Now, discover the roots of the Trayhern brand of courage, as parents Chase and Rachel relive their earliest heartstopping experiences of survival and indomitable love, in

*Dawn of Valor,* Silhouette Special Edition #649.

This February, experience the thrill of LOVE AND GLORY—from the very beginning!

DV-1

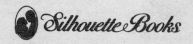
*Silhouette Books*

# Take 4 bestselling love stories FREE

## Plus get a FREE surprise gift!

---

## Special Limited-time Offer

**Silhouette Reader Service®**

Mail to
In the U.S.
3010 Walden Avenue
P.O. Box 1867
Buffalo, N.Y. 14269-1867

In Canada
P.O. Box 609
Fort Erie, Ontario
L2A 5X3

**YES!** Please send me 4 free Silhouette Romance® novels and my free surprise gift. Then send me 6 brand-new novels every month, which I will receive months before they appear in bookstores. Bill me at the low price of $2.25* each. There are no shipping, handling or other hidden costs. I understand that accepting the books and gift places me under no obligation ever to buy any books. I can always return a shipment and cancel at any time. Even if I never buy another book from Silhouette, the 4 free books and the surprise gift are mine to keep forever.

*Offer slightly different in Canada—$2.25 per book plus 69¢ per shipment for delivery. Sales tax applicable in N.Y. Canadian residents add applicable federal and provincial sales tax.

215 BPA HAYY (US)                                    315 BPA 8176 (CAN)

| Name | (PLEASE PRINT) | |
|------|----------------|--|
| Address | | Apt. No. |
| City | State/Prov. | Zip/Postal Code |

This offer is limited to one order per household and not valid to present Silhouette Romance® subscribers. Terms and prices are subject to change.

SROM-BPADR                              © 1990 Harlequin Enterprises Limited

**Silhouette romances are now available in stores at these convenient times each month.**

**Silhouette Desire**
**Silhouette Romance**

These two series will be in stores on the 4th of every month.

**Silhouette Intimate Moments**
**Silhouette Special Edition**

New titles for these series will be in stores on the 16th of every month.

We hope this new schedule is convenient for you. With only two trips each month to your local bookseller, you will always be sure not to miss any of your favorite authors!

## Happy reading!

Please note there may be slight variations in on-sale dates in your area due to differences in shipping and handling.

SDATES